Iced Diamonds

Heather Haven

The Wives of Bath Press

www.thewivesofbath.com

Iced Diamonds © 2012 by Heather Haven

The Wives of Bath Press
5512 Cribari Bend
San Jose, Ca 95135

http:// **www.thewivesofbath.com**

Cover Art © 2013 by Heather Haven
Edited by Baird Nuckolls
Layout and book production by
Heather Haven and Baird Nuckolls

Print ISBN: 978-0-9884086-7-8 (The Wives of Bath Press)
eBook ISBN: 978-0-9884086-8-5 (The Wives of Bath Press)
First eBook edition August, 2012 (Books We Love)

Testimonials

"First of all, I enjoy stories set in the past and Heather Haven's did not disappoint with her well researched setting in history. The main character Persephone Cole was likeable and well rounded. I was drawn into her plight to find a murderer and clear an innocent woman's name from the first page. The plot was easy to follow but complicated enough to keep the reader's attention throughout. …. Definitely a 5 star read for young adults and adults!"

By Killarney Sheffield, author

"In this first chapter, Haven manages to create a cast of characters you immediately connect with and care about: from Percy a street-smart, sarcastic dame with a penchant for Marlene Dietrich-style pant suits and pistachios to her boy-crazy younger sister Serendipity to her daffy mother and more. I don't always like so many characters introduced right away, but Haven did a fine job of giving them just enough interaction that the reader isn't confused.

The other thing I felt the author did well was add in the right amount of detail so that the setting and time period were clear without having to read the book blurb first. I had to chuckle at the plethora of ashtrays around the house to hold pistachio shells. Why it struck me funny I don't know, but it did.

I am eager to see how this mystery plays out. I hope to make time to read this entire book soon. Haven's style of humorous private eye stories continues with this latest endeavor. And I love it!"

Cheryl C. Malandrinos, The Book Connection

The Persephone Cole Vintage Mystery Series:

*The Dagger Before Me – Book One
**Iced Diamonds – Book Two
The Chocolate Kiss-Off – Book Three

*Formerly *Persephone Cole and the Halloween Curse*
**Formerly *Persephone Cole and the Christmas Killings Conundrum*

Dedication

This book is dedicated to my mother, Mary Lee, an original thinker if there ever was one; husband, Norman Meister, who loves strong women; and gutsy broads everywhere who get out there, do what they love, and blaze the trail for the rest of us.

Acknowledgments

I could never do any of this without my writing buddies, in particular, Baird Nuckolls, friend and editor, whose expertise in all things hold me in good stead. Thanks, too, to Robert Goldberg and Jeff Monaghan for help with the cover art. I get by with a little help from my friends!

I love you all.

Iced Diamonds

Chapter One

"Are you that fat lady detective?" The male voice spoke in a hurried manner on the other end of the line.

I don't know about being a lady, Percy thought, *being born and raised on the lower east side, but I am substantial and a PI. So two out of three ain't bad.*

"Yeah, that's me, Persephone Cole. Although, I would have preferred to be called full-figured, plump, stout, portly, hefty, zaftig, rotund, corpulent, chubby, or how about roly-poly? Something with a little thought in it. But who's this and what do you want?" She pulled a small bag of pistachio nuts out of the pocket of her slacks with her free hand, tossed the bag on the telephone table, and routed around for a nut, while she listened.

"My name's Waller, William Waller--"

"Like Fats Waller?" she interrupted, grabbing a salty nut out of the bag. *Okay, you unimaginative creep. We can all make fat cracks.* The other end of the line went stone, cold silent.

Percy popped the nut in her mouth and using years of practice, separated the two shells with her front teeth, and sucked out the meat. She picked the two shells out of her mouth and chewed, as she dropped the shells into one of the ubiquitous ashtrays scattered around the apartment for this sole purpose.

A sudden loud voice coming from the kitchen radio crackled an announcement of the need to buy war bonds. The

United States had been in the war for over a year now and most everyone was tapped out, but the voice droned on, just in case.

"Hold it a minute, Waller," Percy commanded. She cradled the phone against what has been referred to from time to time as her ample bosom, and shouted down the hall of the railroad flat to the kitchen.

"Hey, shut that door, will you, Pop? I got a potential client here." The swinging door swooshed closed between the hallway and the kitchen. Uncle Sam had been muted, at least for the moment.

Percy put the phone back to her ear to the sound of heavy breathing. If she hadn't known better, she would have thought it was an obscene phone call.

"I'm back. What can I do for you, Mr. Waller?" She tried to keep her voice pleasant and professional, but it may have been a little too late for that. She reached for another nut.

"There's a dead elf in my storefront window."

"Excuse me?" Her hand froze midway to her mouth.

"One of those Santa elves from down the street. You know, Santa Land. I want to know what he's doing in my display window."

"Off the top of my head, I'd say not much, him being dead and all." This remark also met stony silence. "Never mind. Have you called the police?" She threw the nut back into the bag.

"Yes, they're here now. I never saw him before." His tone at first sounded puzzled then it changed. 'You're a real smarty pants, aren't you?"

"That's what they tell me." *Never give a jerk an even break, that's my motto.* "So why are you calling me if the cops are taking care of it? How'd you get my number?"

He lowered his voice. "I want to hire you, but I need to talk to you about this in person, not over the phone."

"I don't come cheap, Mr. Waller." *Actually, I do come cheap, but I'm about to hike up the price for you, buster. Fat, huh? We'll see about that.* "I'm twenty a day plus expenses, with a three-day guarantee."

Percy paused, having trouble believing what she was asking, herself, and added, "It being the holiday season and all, I'll make it a two-day guarantee. But it's still twenty bucks a day."

"Very well, Mrs. Cole, whatever you say. Just get here." The words came out rapidly, and in what Miss Schultz, her English teacher, might have called a 'terse manner'.

"It's *Miss* Cole and where's here?"

"Fifty-ninth and Fifth Avenue, right off Central Park. Waller and Sons Jewelry."

"I'll be there as soon as I can."

He paused, mumbled "Thank you," and disconnected.

She cradled the receiver on her shoulder. The last-minute attempt at manners on his part surprised her, even though the address he gave was in a pretty hoity-toity part of Manhattan.

I should have stuck to the three-day minimum.

She hung up the phone with gusto and the rickety telephone table her mother insisted on calling 'dainty' wobbled and nearly fell over. Since she could remember, this genuine knock-off of an exact replica of a Louis the Sixteenth, had been hanging out in the hallway of their lower eastside apartment threatening to collapse. Her mother inherited it from her favorite aunt and despite both women's tender ministrations and conviction of its value; Percy suspected its demise was eminent while its net worth was about thirty-nine cents.

She snatched up the bag of nuts, crammed them in her pocket, turned around in the narrow vestibule and took a quick gander at her reflection in the matching knock-off mirror. The bulge of the nuts only added to the bulges everywhere else. She loved Marlene Dietrich-style pant suits but they only came so big. When last weighed, Percy came in at 172 pounds. At five foot eleven inches, she often piled her hair on top of her head, gaining another three inches of height. This made her taller than any woman she'd met and most of the men serving overseas in Hitler's war games. At thirty-five years of age, Percy preferred to think of herself as impressive, even in her Marlene Dietrich-style pant suit, which had been let down as well as being let out.

A quick scrutiny of her face made her wince. Without makeup, blondish-orange eyebrows and eyelashes looked almost nonexistent. In fact, her unhealthy pasty look was of someone living in a cave, year after year, never seeing the light of day. It was the usual redhead's plight.

One of the best inventions, in Percy's opinion, was cake mascara. She still had hers from high school, circa nineteen twenty-four, a testament to its longevity and her rare usage. Percy toyed with going into the bathroom, lathering it up, and applying some.

Naw, this is good enough for jazz.

She shook her head and long curls trapped in the rubber band at the crown of her head flopped everywhere. Red and amber-streaked ringlets shimmered in the light coming in from the lone window of the vestibule. Even she knew her thick red hair was one of her best features.

But only when it's under control, kiddo, and that's not today; too much moisture in the air. Maybe I can add Pop's fedora to my mop before I leave, so I don't have to think about it.

She headed to the kitchen which bustled with the usual early morning activity. The radio blared in the background, her father sat in his wheelchair with his bad leg resting straight out in its cast and him yelling at her younger sister.

"Serendipity, do you have to do that here?" Pop leaned in as far forward in the wheelchair as his belly and leg would permit. "And while we're eating breakfast? That smell is enough to drop flies. Now put that away. And pay attention to me when I'm talking to you."

Better known as Sera, Percy's kid sister ignored their father and continued to apply red lacquer to short, squat nails. Percy had the same short squat nails and wouldn't dream of bringing attention to them, but that was Sera.

Ignoring the uproar, Mother stood at the stove humming a tuneless but annoying little ditty. Percy's eight-year old son, Oliver, sat at the end of the table, hunched over his oatmeal, short, blue-black hair plastered down from the morning bath. He, too, was paying no attention to the battle of wills going on at the table, lost in the further adventures of the Green Lantern. While he read his comic book, he hummed a similar ditty to that of his grandmother.

Percy tried not to think about her son having inherited her mother's daffiness. Some things are better left alone. She reached up instead, and turned off the radio blasting the Andrew Sister's version of *Don't Sit Under The Apple Tree With Anybody Else But Me.* For an instant, silence reigned. Then everyone started to talk again.

"Sorry, Pop." Sera's voice was, however, devoid of any contrition. She tossed dyed blond curls. "But I have to get to the factory by eight and I won't have any time to polish my nails after work. I've got a big date tonight."

"How lovely." Mother spoke in a dreamy tone, the only one she used when awake. "So many young men you see, Serendipity, and nearly every evening. Have I met this new boy, what's his name?"

Sera didn't answer.

"She probably can't remember his name, grandma," Oliver said in a guileless tone, without looking up from his comic book.

"Out of the mouths of babes," muttered Percy.

Mother turned from the stove and dumped a large dollop of hot oatmeal into an empty bowl before an empty chair. Percy sat down and picked up a spoon.

"I'm in a hurry, Mother, so nothing else for me." Percy poured diluted, condensed milk over the warm cereal. She hated oatmeal and loathed canned milk, but neither eggs nor bacon had seen the inside of their kitchen in months. "Pop, I just got a job." She shoveled in a large spoonful of the cereal, trying not to taste it.

Everyone except Oliver turned and stared her. Money being tight and Pop unable to work with his broken leg, it left Percy to be the major bread winner of the family. They were having what President Roosevelt referred to as 'lean times.'

Pop was the first to speak. "What kind of a job? Is that what the phone call was about? You know, we don't take just any job." He raised his hand, pointing his index finger at the ceiling before making his further statement. "Cole Investigations has standards."

"Pop, it's a jeweler on Fifth Avenue. This Waller guy seems like a real jerk, but who am I to say no? Something about a dead elf left in his store window, and the cops are already there. It sounds in and out, but I did manage to get a two-day guarantee." She looked around at the rapt attention her remarks had drawn. "And, I'm making twenty bucks a day plus expenses."

"Twenty bucks?" Oliver looked up from his comic book, astonishment written all over his sweet, freckled face. "A day?"

"Oh, my," remarked her mother, doing her usual Zazu Pitts impression. "So much money! And for one day! Why, our rent is only nine dollars and we live here thirty days out of the month, sometimes thirty-one. Isn't that right, Father?" Mother stopped stirring the pot of oatmeal, turned, and glanced at her husband for support.

Used to his wife's zaniness, Pop looked at her and smiled. "It is, indeed, Mother."

"And in February, it's twenty-eight," murmured Sera, blowing on her nails.

Their parents had called each other 'Mother' and 'Father' since Percy could remember. Probably because Pop was named after Habakkuk, a biblical prophet. Mother's real name was Lamentation. With her willowy shape and long, white blonde hair, Mother looked more like a Dandelion, threatening to blow away at any moment.

Percy's family had a history of unusual, if not downright peculiar, first names on both sides. Her older brother's name was Adjudication, and no doubt the main reason he'd become a lawyer. So, stuck with Adjudication, Serendipity, and Persephone, the Cole off-spring was glad for the usage of nicknames, such as Jude, Sera, and Percy.

"I don't want you to put yourself in jeopardy on this job, not even for a king's ransom, Persephone." Pop turned back to his eldest daughter. "If I could go with you --"

"Don't worry, Pop," she interrupted. "Like I said, this should be in and out and the fastest twenty bucks - no, make that forty bucks – Cole Investigations ever made." She gulped down the last of her breakfast, got up, and took the car keys off the hook by the back door.

"Think Ophelia has enough gas in her to get me midtown, Pop?" The 1929 Dodge was the family car, old, black, and ugly, but its engine came to life each time you pressed down on the starter. The gas gauge was one of the many things that no longer worked, and between rationing and only being able to afford to put in one or two gallons at a time, father and daughter ran out of gas more times than they cared to think about.

"Put in five gallons, Persephone, right before my leg turned bad."

"That was two months ago." She gave it some thought. "Man, has it been that long?"

Pop smiled. "Nobody else driving it now except you."

"I would if Pop would let me," Sera interjected, with a pout.

"You got all those boyfriends to tote you around, Serendipity. You don't need a car." Pop's voice was kind but firm.

"Well, the last time I got home on fumes." Percy gave out a laugh and shook her head. "I'd better take the subway. It's faster, anyway." One thing about living on the lower eastside, a couple of blocks walk to the BMT and it got you nearly everywhere in Manhattan.

"Get off at fifty-seventh and Fifth." Pop talked as if she hadn't ridden the train a thousand times. "And good luck with the job."

"I'm taking your fedora, Pop. My hair's a wreck. Hope you don't mind." She snatched the hat off the rack near the back door then ran to the end of the table, reached over and tousled her son's short, damp hair. "You be a good boy and do everything Grandma says, Oliver. Don't forget your raincoat. And come straight home from school. Okay?"

He dropped his comic book and grinned up at her, the child who gave her life meaning. "Okay, Mommy." He screwed his face up, closed his eyes, and she placed a noisy, wet kiss on his forehead.

"You're just so yummy, I could eat you up just like a pistachio nut." Percy grabbed him in a bear hug and pretended to smother him. He giggled and so did everyone at the table. She left to the sounds of laughter.

Chapter Two

"It's around here somewhere." He crossed the room with a wheeze. "And when I find it, I'm going to blow up the building. Who do they think they are selling my place out from under me?"

He threw an empty beer keg across the basement floor. It banged down, bounced three times then scuttled along the uneven floor, resting near piles of stacked boxes lining one long wall. Though the keg was no longer moving, the noise continued to reverberate in the dank, cluttered cement room. He looked up to the ceiling with fear.

"I need to be careful," he told the dog, sitting in a corner. "I don't want anyone to hear me until it's time, until I find it. Too bad about the little fellow, but he shouldn't have come snooping around."

He lifted the kerosene lamp and screwed up his eyes, trying to see in the dim lighting. "So many boxes." He looked back to where the dog, crouched in the corner, its scared eyes reflecting the scant light. "Come here boy, I won't hurt you. Maybe you can help me find it."

The wary dog crept forward, half-wagging his tail more in hope than in promise.

Chapter Three

Thirty minutes later Percy arrived at the Fifty-seventh and Fifth subway stop, resurfaced to street level, and walked the two blocks uptown to the jewelry store. Even if Waller and Sons Jewelry hadn't been her destination, she would have lingered there, drawn in by the huge crowd and general hub-bub taking place on the sidewalk. Two cop cars and a meat wagon were scrunched between a bus stop and a red fire hydrant.

You one of these guys, you can park wherever you want.

She walked inside but paused at the doorway, coming along side Sergeant Tom O'Leary, a guy she'd been pals with since the fifth grade. Even then she knew he'd be a cop, joined later by his kid brother, Jimmy, when he was old enough. When you're Irish, you become a cop, priest, or bartender. Both boys weren't particularly religious and didn't drink.

Behind him, seven or eight other boys in blue moved around the plush showroom, decorated in shades of pale yellow and money. They were looking for anything out of place, but diamond infested glass cases kept getting in their way.

"Hey, Percy." Tom broke out with an amiable grin. "Shopping for a sparkler?"

"Yeah, my other rocks got dirty, so I threw them away. I need a new set."

They smiled at each other the way long-time friends do.

If I'd had the sense God gave a lemon, I would have married Tom when I had the chance instead of the idiot who took a powder when he found out I was pregnant. Then she remembered why she didn't marry Tom. *Lots of like, no love.*

"How's the wife, Tom?"

"About to drop the seventh."

"You got to find another hobby, pal." She smacked him on the arm and he laughed.

She looked behind Tom and knew why she was there. Detective Kenneth Hutchers scribbled notes while a thin, balding, and stooped-over man talked, bobbing his head up and down in nervous jerks. Something told her the stoop was her client. With a nod to Tom, she ambled over, pulled out her bag of nuts, and started the removal routine with her teeth, while she eavesdropped on their conversation.

"So what time did you arrive here?" Hutchers' voice was low in volume but powerful in intent.

"I've already told you."

The man had a nervous, exasperated air to him, but there was something else, something Percy couldn't quite place. Whatever it was, it was all he could do to contain himself and answer the questions being thrown at him. Percy watched him the way you do a pot of water about to boil over.

"Seven-thirty. I always open early on Mondays to check stock and see what needs to be reordered. Where's my daughter? I need to find my daughter."

Hutchers ignored the question and went right on. "And that's when you found him? When you opened the door?"

"No, as I said before, officer, I -"

"Detective. Detective Hutchers," Hutchers interrupted.

"Detective Hutchers." The jeweler repeated the name, his eyes blinking rapidly. "I...I knew just looking at the window something was wrong. The display case was in disarray and then I saw him. There he was, in the middle of my garlands and bells, the little Christmas tree lying on top of him." Waller gestured to the laden gurney and the three of them turned in that direction.

Percy got her first look-see at the victim, and it would have been funny if he wasn't quite so dead. The size of a six-year old child, but with a larger torso, neck and head, he was dressed from head to foot in a bright green leotard. Elongated, emerald feet pointed upward, the ends of the shoes curling into a semi-circle, two red balls dangling from the tips. He wore a green felt Robin Hood type hat, tasseled with another red ball, as large as a small balloon. He had a handsome face, even in death, with a five o'clock shadow dotting a strong jaw line even Superman would have envied.

Wait a minute. I've been reading too many of Oliver's comic books. Come back from kiddy land to Santa Land.

She dropped a handful of empty shells in her pocket, stepped closer and noticed the small lines around the elf's closed eyes and grim mouth. He looked around her age and, like her, no longer in his first youth, as they would say. Of course, he was no longer in anything.

Hutchers' voice caused Percy to swivel back to the jeweler and the head cop. "So you finally got here, Perce. Took you long enough. You know William Waller? The son in Waller and Son Jewelers."

"Yes, my father is retired and it's my business now." He reached out a weak hand and she took it into a strong shake. He winced. "How do you do Mrs. Cole?"

"*Miss* Cole. Sorry we're not meeting under better circumstances, Mr. Waller," she added. *There, I can be as civil as the next person.* She even smiled at Hutchers, who returned the smile with a glare. He had a lot to glare about these days.

Percy's brother, Jude, handled Hutchers messy divorce a few months back. He'd had a wife who wanted everything, including his jockey shorts, but not what was in them. Jude

managed to get him visitation rights to the kids and keep his car, a '39 Desoto, so Hutchers was a grateful man.

"Excuse us a minute, Mr. Waller." Hutchers yanked at Percy by her upper arm.

"Hey! Watch the suit. I just got it yesterday."

Ignoring Percy's command, Hutchers hauled her to a glass counter holding diamond solitaire engagement rings, several of them large enough to choke a horse. She shrugged free of the detective and looked back at Waller.

He is one worried man. No, not worried. Scared. This man is terrified something is going to come out. This is interesting.

Out of earshot, Hutchers said, "Listen, Perce, I don't have a lotta time, so here's the skinny." He never called her Persephone or Percy, but shortened her name to one syllable, as if saying more than that was too much effort. He went on, "Waller finds the dead dwarf, calls us, we find his daughter's handbag lying underneath the guy --"

"That would be Waller's daughter's handbag, right? Not the dead dwarf's."

"What are you, a comedian? Why would I tell Waller to call you if it wasn't his daughter I'm talking about?"

"Just making sure, Hutchers. Checking the facts. You don't have to bite my head off."

"Well, shut up and let me finish."

"So finish."

For some reason her retort appeased him. "Okay. So we open the purse, Perce, and we find a snub nose, recently fired."

"I take it the elf was shot."

I'm not going to say anything about the double purses. No point in further annoying an already pissed off guy.

"You're getting quicker. So we ask Daddy where the daughter is and he don't know, nobody does. It isn't certain, but I'd say by how stiff the stiff is, he was probably shot sometime around three or four in the morning. Waller, by the way, has a crackerjack alibi until seven-thirty this morning. He was spending the night playing cards with his good pal, Mayor Fiorello LaGuardia, along with about a dozen other prominent citizens. Now there's an alibi. But the girl, his daughter, what's her name." He looked at his notes. "Lily Waller, she don't show up for work this morning. She works at Santa Land along with the dead guy. I got a warrant out for her arrest. That's it."

"That her purse over there?" Percy pointed to a small silver bag lying on the counter, with a tag on it. The chainmail clutch bag looked like it was made out of real silver. A large chunk of jade carved in the shape of a dragon decorated the clasp. Two glittering red stones filled the eyes, probably rubies. "Looks expensive."

He shrugged. "She's a rich doll. These people always think they're above the law."

She turned her head around and studied the father.

With your attitude, Hutchers, no wonder her father looks scared. Or worse.

Percy turned back to Hutchers. He was glaring at her again, eyebrows furrowed, lips pinched.

"One of these days your face is going to freeze like that and then you'll be sorry." Startled, Hutchers' expression changed to one of confusion. "Never mind. Just something a mother gets used to saying to her kid. It's in the handbook. You tell him I was fat?"

"Yeah, something like that. I don't want him thinking you was no flimsy girl, can't take care of herself. Now look, I owe your brother big time, and he said he would appreciate it if I could do something for his sister – and yes, that would be *you* and not the dead dwarf's sister – so I'm doing it. What with your father laid up and all, I'm being a good guy. But I don't need no lip from my department over this, right? So just pretend you're interested in helping him out, make a few bucks, and go back down to the east side." He leaned in and

glared at her again, this time eyeball to eyeball. He was her height, so he could do it. "But don't get in my way, understand?"

You can be one nasty, rude slob, copper. I hope Santa leaves coal in your stocking.

She threw him an outward smile. He didn't return it. "Understood, Hutchers," she said. "Thanks for the job and Merry Christmas. Have a pistachio." She proffered the bag. He ignored her gesture.

"Don't mention it, Perce. And I mean that. Don't mention it to nobody or we'll both be sorry."

Each word was stressed, as if she was too stupid to get it, otherwise. Then the charm school drop-out turned around and went back to Waller, who was gnawing on his nails like he hadn't eaten in a week. Percy followed and came to the jeweler's side.

Hutchers ignored Percy but looked at the jewelry store owner and closed his notebook.

"That's it for now. I'll let you know when we find your daughter, unless she turns herself in first. You might want to tell her that if she comes by or calls. It would look better for her. My men will be finished up here in about an hour. Then you can straighten up and open for business."

"Thank you." Waller said, once again throwing in some manners. Somebody may be dead, but he was going to be genteel about it. Together Percy and the jeweler watched Hutchers storm out of the shop, as if the crime had been a personal affront to him.

Waller moved around behind a long, glass counter decorated with crystal bowls filled with red and green Christmas balls, and toward a narrow door at the back of the room. He gestured for Percy to follow.

The door opened to a short hallway, at the end of which stood a steel-grated, glass door leading to a back alley. Off to one side of the hall were two doors, one closed and one open. The opened door was a bathroom, with an overhead, low-watt bulb throwing a modicum of light in the tiny space. Waller reached up and pulled on the chain, shutting off the light. Then he opened an opposite door, which appeared to be his office. All the while he said nothing and neither did Percy.

A small desk, two comfortable-looking brown leather chairs, and dozens of black velvet-covered jewelry boxes filled the small room. On the windowsill a philodendron struggled for life, looking thirsty and neglected. The window also wore steel grating. She could see where being in the diamond business needed a lot of protective steel.

"Sit down, Miss Cole." He sat behind the desk in one leather chair and she sat in the other facing him.

"Okay, so I'm here," she said, getting right to it. "What do you want?"

"I need you to find Lily before the police do or before she does anything else."

"Meaning what? You think she killed the elf?"

"Of course not. Lily's not violent, not really. It's only she can be…she's a bit… a bit headstrong and…" He stopped talking and looked down at his gnawed fingernails.

"And?"

"I guess I should say it. She sometimes does irresponsible things. Her mother died when she was seven and she never got over it. That's all."

He looked over at an eight by ten studio portrait framed in silver. Percy's eyes followed his gaze. She considered the picture of a glamorous, young brunette, wearing heavy make-up and a Vaselined, vapid smile. Her youth coupled with his fatherly look of adoration told Percy this was the jeweler's daughter, even though Waller hadn't said so. Lily's ears were garnished with two diamond drop earrings, set with stones larger than most of the marbles Percy had seen her son playing with from his collection. Waller broke away from the photo, cleared his throat, and began

picking up square, velvet ring cases. He stacked them neatly at one end of the desk.

"What else, Mr. Waller? I'm happy to take your money but you might want to get something for it. Let's start with the gun. Is it hers?" She lifted a pistachio to her mouth, bit down and separated the shell from the nut.

He didn't say anything but nodded, lining up the small boxes in three or four stacks.

"How old is Lily?"

"Eighteen just. Last week was her birthday."

"That's pretty young to be carrying."

"Being in the diamond business has its downsides, Miss Cole. One of them is robbery. We've been robbed three or four times at gunpoint and once, they tried to take Lily as a hostage, a bargaining chip. She was fifteen. She got away but I gave her some protection to carry after that."

"She went to school carrying a piece?" Percy was dumbfounded and didn't bother to hide it. *If my son carried a gun to school, fifteen or fifty, I'd kill him.*

"Lily dropped out of school at fourteen, in the middle of term. I couldn't get her to go back. I've hired tutors for her from time to time, for all the good it does me."

"Okay, so Lily's a handful. What else?"

"A few weeks ago Lily took a job at Santa Land as a lark. She didn't need the money. Then I found out she…ah… knew this….ah…elf. Conrad was his name, Conrad Wilson. She'd been hired to be one of Santa's helpers, so they worked together, sort of. Anyway, I found them together at our Long Island estate." He hesitated and looked away, fidgeting with a long, black velvet box, probably meant to hold a necklace worth more than the state of Delaware.

"In flagrante delicto?"

She'd learned this phrase along with others from several of her brother's books she'd studied on the law. A

private detective should know a few things, including which end of a gun to point and fire.

He nodded and went back to stacking boxes.

"She at the Long Island estate now or you think she skipped town?"

"No, I think she's there. I phoned but no one answered. The staff is on holiday and the house is empty. Her car is missing and I can't think of anywhere else she'd go. She loves that house. It's the only place she'd known with her mother."

"You want me to go there and talk her into turning herself in?" He nodded again. "If you think she's there, why don't you go, yourself?" Percy looked around, found an ashtray and dropped several shells into it. "And stop with the boxes. Please."

He hesitated, set the boxes down, and leaned forward looking directly into her eyes. "I'm sorry. I guess I'm nervous."

"You don't look nervous to me. More like scared. You scared, Mr. Waller?"

"I..I..yes, I am. Lily can be…can be…" He seemed to search for the right words.

"A handful," Percy offered.

William Waller nodded. "She can be, yes. Miss Cole, for all the men she's had in her life, including me and her grandfather, she's never trusted any of us. I don't know why. Maybe I should have spent more time with her when she was little, but my business takes me away a lot. Lately, I've tried my best to win her over. For God's sake, I'm her father. But she doesn't seem to…respond to men except romantically, and that never lasts long. I'm hoping you, as an older woman, can win her confidence. That's why I asked the detective if he knew any older policewomen. He didn't, but suggested you."

Man, oh, man. When the hell did I become 'an older' woman? Merry Christmas to me. Look who's got the lump of coal now.

"Maybe Lily will open up to you," the jeweler went on, unaware of Percy's thoughts. "If nothing else, maybe you can get her to go to the police before they hunt her down. I didn't tell them about Long Island, just the apartment in Beekman Place."

"That doesn't give us much time. The cops aren't as dumb as you'd like to think. Write down the address." Percy did some fast thinking. *The only way I can get to Long island quick enough is by car. And if I'm going to do that, I need gas money.*

"I'm going to need a cash advance," Percy said matter-of-factly.

The jeweler nodded, drew out a set of keys from his pocket, opened a locked drawer in the bottom of the desk, and hauled out a metal box. Using another key, he opened the box to reveal more lettuce than she'd seen in her life. He picked up a pile of what she first thought was tens and twenties. He flipped over the stack to reveal one-hundred dollar bills. She tried to keep her eyebrows from banging into the fedora plopped on her head. Waller peeled off three bills.

"Here's three-hundred dollars." He slid over a pad and fountain pen. "I'll need a receipt."

So you were expecting a five spot, Percy, instead of three C notes. Get over it and try to keep from stuttering when you open your mouth.

"Okay." With a shaking hand, she scrawled the amount and her name on the paper while he continued talking.

"If you can save my daughter from this…and from herself…I'll give you another one-thousand dollars. Keep her out of jail and I'll make it five-thousand."

Five thousand bucks! Enough to get my own house, my own car, live on my own, just Oliver and me! She took a deep breath. *Slow down, kiddo, you haven't earned it yet. Besides, maybe he's talking through his hat.*

"You want to put that down in writing? And sign it?" She returned the bag of nuts to her pocket, but threw more shells into the ashtray.

"Of course." He reached for a large notepad and began to write. "I don't know how legal this is."

"Legal enough." Percy watched him write one or two sentences and sign his name at the bottom. She reached over, took the note, folded it and put it in her breast pocket. "Let me suggest you get yourself a good criminal lawyer. If you don't know one, my brother probably does."

Mr. Waller shook his head. "I don't want it to go that far. She didn't kill the man."

"Regardless, line somebody up. Or call my brother, Jude, Jude Cole. He's an attorney and he's honest. That's why he's broke. He's in the phone book." She stood. "I'd better get going. If I know Hutchers, he'll be on this like a drunk on a beer. Got a glass of water?"

A little thrown, Waller nonetheless reached over to a tumbler filled with water and poured some into one of the glasses resting on a nearby tray. She took the glass, crossed the small room over to the windowsill. Percy poured a steady stream of water into the philodendron, neither Waller nor she saying a word.

The bought and paid for detective turned back to her client. "Things die from neglect, Mr. Waller, or sometimes they shoot somebody. We're going to see if that's what your daughter did."

Chapter Four

"I can't find it, boy," the man said to the dog. "But it's here. We'll look again tomorrow." He strained his eyes to look at the watch on his wrist, drawing from the negligible light of the lamp.

"I got to go up and mop the store. It won't look right if I don't get up to the store." He clawed at the rummaged goods he'd strewn about on the floor, chucking them in a corner, so he could have a pathway. "Putting it back, boy, so it looks like nobody's been here. Not that anybody comes down here. Nobody's got the key." His face clouded over. Even in the half light, the dog saw the change and skulked away.

"Of course, that didn't keep that elf out. Nosy bastard, but he got his. He got his." He looked around in the darkness for the dog and called out loudly. "Come on, boy. We got to get upstairs."

Chapter Five

The trip over the Long Island turnpike was fast and quiet. At midday, there weren't a lot of cars on the road and gas rationing was at its peak. Ophelia sailed along the road, steady and solid. Percy loved this old car, even the butterfly window that wouldn't close and made driving a windy experience, and downright frigid in the winter.

She had to laugh when she thought of the shocked expression on the gas jockey's face at the neighborhood gas station when she told him to 'fill 'er up.' The Cole's usual limit was 3-gallons at a time. Maybe things were changing for the Coles.

Good God, I hope so. This being broke all the time is getting on my nerves.

The scenery shifted from cement grey streets and red brick buildings to mostly trees and foliage, dressed down for the winter. It hadn't snowed yet but had rained mightily and the rain-soaked terrain looked bleak and sad. Percy shivered and turned on the heater, hoping it might kick in. It didn't.

Percy removed the slip of paper with the directions from the right breast pocket of her suit when she reached the Nassau County line. She'd heard about Sands Point, where the swells lived, but had never met anybody with enough greenbacks to live there. The people she knew struggled for every dime and came from the tenements or Flat Bush.

A glimpse of her reflection in the rearview mirror made Percy wish she'd taken time to comb her hair. She tucked a wisp of a curl back into the crown of the hat, pulled down the brim, and looked back at the road.

Hanging a right off Middle Neck Road onto Tideway, a long row of filigreed wrought iron fences appeared. Ornate gates worthy of ushering in fancy schmancy cars stood sentinel in front of wide driveways. In varying shades of gold, black or grey cast iron metal, they shielded the sloping lawns and set-back mansions from the uninvited and riff-raff, such as her. From what she saw on the map, the other side of the mansions hovered near the Long Island Sound, within skipping distance of moored sailboats and yachts. Five years previous, a hurricane had struck Long Island, the likes of which no one expected. Fire Island was totally submerged, and a lot of the stately dwellings she passed had six-feet of water dancing on their marble and oak ballroom floors instead of somebody's well-shod tootsies.

You couldn't pay me to live out here. She clucked self-righteously. *Give me a fourth floor walk-up anytime. Well, maybe not a fourth floor walk-up, because I'd like a yard for Oliver to play in, but it has to be in the City, for crying out loud. Someday we'll have our own place, maybe in Chelsea, just the two of us. Five grand could make it happen. I'll make it happen.*

Finding the address she needed, she pulled into an oyster-shelled driveway, tires crackling her arrival, and came to a stop in front of a wrought iron gate wearing the initials WW in seven foot high letters. A sharp wind smelling of salty, cold air with an overlay of fish blew the broken butterfly window open, blasting her in the face. She pushed the small pane closed, only to have it blown open again, when she released her hand.

She looked around the sparse, neat interior of the car for a string, twine or rope, something similar to the one attached, now frayed and broken by the strain of the constant wind.

Where the hell's a rubber band when you need one?

Frustrated, she searched the seats of the car then leaned over to look on the floorboard. Her hat fell off and curls cascaded down and in her face. *Wait a minute!* She reached up and yanked at the rubber band containing her high ponytail. With hurried movements, she secured the band around the knob on the frame and the handle of the window. It held fast.

She twisted her hair on top of her head and slammed on the hat, pulling it down as far as it would go, and checked the results in the rearview mirror.

I look ridiculous. Her ears jutted out and she had no forehead to speak of. *But the hat should stay on, even in the gale-force winds kicking up outside.*

Scanning the double gate for a latch, Percy spotted it, got out, and gave it a twist open. Percy pushed at both gates and, aided by the wind, they spread apart and smacked against the back side of the fence. She returned to the car, drove through, toying with the idea of shutting the gates.

Nope. All things being equal, sweetie, you might need to make a hasty retreat.

Though the rain had stopped hours ago, dripping, leafless trees lining either side of the driveway still looked depressed and ominous. Percy followed the driveway to the front of a three-story red-brick house, where the drive offered either the five-car garage as a resting place or made a circle that looped back onto itself. She stopped the car in front of the house, leaned over to the passenger's side, and looked out.

Holy cow! I've seen hotels smaller than this. I'm glad I put on matching socks.

She hopped out of the car and shivered, wishing she'd worn her coat. It had to be at least fifteen degrees colder here than in the City. Turning her head to give her a full view of both the grounds and the front of the house, she noted that the place looked deserted. Between the lack of vegetation and the weather, she'd seen happier-looking graveyards.

The curved front steps had been painted an austere white. The massive front door sported a large fir wreath dotted with holly and pinecones. It was the only human touch she could see. The Christmas wreath had been painted gold - *like all of it, baby* -- in the same gilding as her mother's table and mirror. Even the ribbon had a veneered, stiff look. Percy took a moment to stare at the wreath then shook her head.

I don't know, this must be me. What's with all the tacky gold?

She raised her hand to ring the doorbell when the door burst open, startling her. On the other side of the threshold, a young brunette, equally startled, stood holding a small, blue leather overnight case in one hand. At her side, a large matching piece of luggage sat on a black and white checked marble floor, waiting for her to have a free hand to pick it up.

Like most people who are surprised, both women momentarily stood staring and frozen in place, one with a hand reaching down for luggage, the other woman reaching for the doorbell.

Percy recovered first. Even though the girl no longer had a face painted like a Hoochie Coochie dancer, Percy knew the owner of this clean, but blotchy mug was Lily. Further, the girl dressed in a dark green wool coat, matching wide brimmed felt hat set back from her tear-stained face, was obviously making a run for it – thus the luggage.

Percy reached forward with the same hand she was going to use to ring the bell. The movement caused the girl to screech, wheel around, and dashed back inside the house.

"Hey, wait a minute! Lily! I need to talk to you!" Percy followed her and snatched at the first thing she could grab hold of, the back of the girl's coat collar. "Your father sent me. I'm here to help you," she tried to say over the screaming.

"Leave me alone! Don't hurt me! Let me go!" Lily dropped the case, pivoting and twirling in place in an effort to break free, all the while shrieking at the top of her voice.

Surmising the five-foot two- girl didn't weigh more than a hundred pounds, Percy wrapped a solid arm around Lily's body and lifted her in the air.

"Jeesh, all right, already," said Percy. "Shut up, will you, and I'll let you go. What's the matter with you?"

Instead of answering, Lily stopped struggling, but reached back over her head. She made contact with Percy's hat and ripped it off, pulling out hunks of red hair.

"Ow!" Stunned, Percy dropped the girl, who turned around and kicked Percy as hard as she could in the shin. The older woman let out a cry of pain and bent over her injured leg. Long red curls, freed from their imprisonment, tousled every which way, some touching the floor.

"Oh, no," Lily cried out. "You're not a man, you're a woman." She stood staring in wonderment at the wounded woman bowed over, rubbing her shin.

"Ow! Criminy, sister, of course I'm a woman!" A pain riddled face stared back at the young one's then broke out in a smile. She straightened up and looked down. "You thought I was a man?"

The girl gave a stiff nod, as if embarrassed.

"That's funny." Percy threw her head back and laughed then stopped mid-chuckle. "No it's not." She looked directly into Lily's face, searching her eyes. "You were scared because you thought I was a man?"

Lily didn't answer but burst into tears, bringing hands to her face and sobbing noisily into them. Great gulping sounds wracked her small body.

"All right, all right, all right. Stop it," Percy demanded. Putting aside the throbbing of her shin, she grabbed Lily by the top of the coat sleeve, much the way Hutchers had grabbed her, and dragged her to a nearby seating area.

"Okay, sit down, kid."

Lily obeyed, dropping herself into a red and wine embroidered high back chair. She looked young and miserable. Percy sat in a matching chair facing the girl and stared at her.

"You *are* Lily Waller, right?"

The girl nodded but didn't look up.

"My name is Persephone Cole and I'm a private detective. My friends call me Percy but you can call me Miss Cole. You hear me say your father sent me to help you?"

The girl nodded again but turned away. Now she looked more scared than miserable. She started to cry again.

"Okay, stop that. And I mean it." Percy used her brusque and no nonsense voice. "We don't have time for tears, so cut it out."

Lily stopped sobbing, but still wouldn't look at Percy.

"That's better. We need to talk and we need to do it quick. The cops are going to be here any minute."

Lily looked up at Percy, horror written all over her face. "The police? Here?"

"That's right."

"Then I've got to get away!" She started to rise, but Percy reached over and shoved her back in the chair.

"Not so fast. I'll help you get away but, I have one question first and you're going to look me in the eye and tell me the truth." Percy leaned forward, sharp, green eyes staring into swollen, brown ones. "I've got an eight-year old son, so I know a lie when I hear one, okay? Look at me now. Look at me."

Hesitantly, almost as if against her will, Lily looked into Percy's cool, assessing eyes.

"You kill that elf?"

Lily didn't reply, but clenched her jaw, her lips set in a thin, tight line. She shook her head adamantly.

"That's good, but I'm going to ask you again and this time, you answer me out loud. Did you kill that man?"

"No, no, I swear it." Lily's voice, unlike before, was low and calm. She sat up in the chair, suddenly revitalized, almost energetic. Words came tumbling out. "I don't know what happened. I was only gone for a few minutes. When I came back, I found him shot! He was lying in the window, eyes open, blood everywhere. I swear on my dead mother's grave I didn't do it." With those last words, she buried her face in her hands but didn't cry this time. Maybe the dark felt good.

Percy studied the girl. "All right, I believe you." She looked around. "Anybody else here? Anyone know you're here?"

Lily looked up and said, "No, everyone's gone. I --"

Percy stood, interrupted Lily. "Then get up and let's get going."

The girl stood but didn't move. "Where --?"

"I'll tell you in the car." Percy limped over and picked her hat up from the floor. "Jesus, those shoes are lethal."

"I'm sorry --"

"Never mind. Grab the little bag and let's get out of here." Percy plopped the fedora back on her head, picked up the large suitcase in front of the still-open door, and turned to the girl. "What the hell you got in here, bricks?"

"Books, mostly." Lily ran to the overnight kit, lying on its side. As she bent over to retrieve it she said, "But where are we going?"

"Some place safe. At least for now."

Lily walked toward Percy but hesitated after a few steps.

"Lily," Percy said, running out of patience, "we both got a lot riding on keeping you out of jail, but you move it right now or you're on your own. Your call."

The girl practically flew past Percy, out the door, and down the steps. "Is this your car?"

"It is. Get in." Percy opened the back door on the driver's side and slid the suitcase on the backseat, while Lily clamored into the passenger's seat. After she slammed her

own door shut, Percy started the engine and turned to her passenger.

"How were you planning on getting away from here? You call a cab or --"

Now it was Lily's turn to interrupt Percy. "I've got my own car. It's in the garage. I was going to drive to Canada, somewhere, anywhere."

Percy nodded, saying nothing. She followed the circular drive, heading toward the exit and looked over at Lily. "What kind of trees are those?"

Confused, the girl looked out the window at the passing scenery, searching the terrain.

"The drippy ones."

Lily shook her head. "I don't know. Is it important?"

Percy shrugged. "Not really. Just curious. They're so damned ugly, I wondered why anyone would deliberately plant them."

"They're pretty in the summer," Lily said, her voice soft and far away, as if she was remembering a time when trees had leaves on them and there were no dead elves.

Percy drove past the gates, put the car in neutral and opened the car door. "I'll be right back. I'm going to close the gates."

Lily nodded absentmindedly, still lost in her reverie. Gates closed, Percy got back into the car, just as it began to rain heavily again.

Jeesh, I hope the windshield wipers work, they've been shorting out. Oh, the hell with it, I've got more important things to worry about. If I have to, I'll stick my head out the window.

They drove in silence for several blocks, windshield wipers tapping nicely. The sound of police sirens, faint at first, got louder and louder, until Percy saw flashing lights coming at them on the other side of the road. She slowed down, pulled over, and came to a complete stop on the median. Black and white police cars, three of them, whizzed by.

"Well, I think we know where that parade is heading." Percy chuckled to herself.

"Do you think they saw us?" Lily's head whipped around, her voice anxious and strained.

"In this downpour? They're lucky they can see ten feet ahead of them." Percy looked at her young charge before getting back onto the road. "Okay, Lily, time to tell me what happened."

"Oh, God, must I?" Lily sounded drained of life. She shook her head and leaned against the car door. "I'm so tired."

"Rest later, talk now. I need to know what happened; I'm sticking my neck out for you." *For you and five thousand clams, but I don't have to go into that.* "What were you doing in your father's store at three o'clock in the morning?" The silent girl stared out the window. "Lily?"

"Do I have to say? I...I'm...I don't want --"

"Listen, honey, a man's been bumped off. He may have been wearing one silly getup, but he's dead. The cops are looking to pin it on you. You better start talking."

"All right." She let out a deep sigh but continued to lean against the door. "Connie and I..."

"That's Conrad Barnes, right?"

"Yes, his nickname was Connie. It's usually a girl's name, but it was his."

"I know something about wrong gender nicknames, but go on."

"Anyway, Connie thought it would be fun to... to...have relations in Dad's store window in the middle of the night in our Santa Land costumes."

"You mean sex?"

"Yes."

Percy glanced at her. "In the store window? On fifth Avenue?" Even she could hear the school marm tone in her voice.

"I know how it sounds, what you must be thinking, but it was all in fun. He was a fun sort of person." She wiped away tears on her face. "I really liked him." Lily became silent.

Percy's eyes turned back to the road. Large drops of water splashed on the windshield with noisy precision. Thankfully, the wipers continued to work. The car hit a deep puddle and slowed it down. Two huge arcs of water splayed out on either side of the vehicle. Percy took her foot off the accelerator, reducing the speed to twenty-five miles an hour, and pumped the brakes to dry them off. She looked at her watch.

High noon. At this rate, we won't get back to the City for at least an hour. It can all still work. I'll make it work.

"Kid, I'm not good with this silence," she said to Lily. "Keep talking. How'd you get into the store and at what time?"

"We got there around two, two-thirty. I used my keys --"

"You've got keys to your father's store?"

"Sure. It will come to me some day."

"If you say so. Go on."

"I opened the door, turned off the alarm, and Connie and I started fooling around, you know." Lily began to draw on the foggy window, little circles and squares. "After a few minutes, I started feeling sick. I've been throwing up a lot lately. I think I've got the flu or something."

Or maybe there's a rabbit out there somewhere about to die in a pregnancy test. I wonder if you use protection when you have your 'relations.' Shut up, Percy.

Lily stopped drawing on the window and sat bolt upright. "So I went into the bathroom in the back and vomited. I can't have been gone for more than ten minutes. And when I came back, I saw him…Connie…Oh, it's too horrible."

"Before you start to cry again, did you hear anything? A noise? Something unusual or different." She glanced over and saw Lily shaking her head in sad jerky motions, wiping away the flowing tears with quivering fingers.

"And you didn't see anyone, either? Someone out on the sidewalk or something?"

"No, no, no." For the first time, Lily exhibited impatience and anger. "I never saw or heard anything. I'd closed the bathroom door, and I was pretty noisy myself."

"What about the hallway door? Did you close that one, too?"

"Let me think. Yes, yes I did. I didn't want Connie to hear me. Just thinking about it makes me want to vomit again."

"Well, you better give me plenty of warning. I just cleaned this car out."

Lily nodded but didn't answer.

"Why didn't you take your purse with you when you bolted?"

"I couldn't find it. I looked everywhere."

"The cops found it under the body and it had your recently fired gun in it."

"Oh, God." Lily bit her lower lip.

Percy glanced at the girl. "How'd you get home if you couldn't find your purse? Weren't your car keys in there?"

"No, I always leave them in the ignition. Otherwise, I lose them."

"You could lose your car that way." Once again, the school marm came out in Percy. She'd have to watch that.

Lily didn't reply but shrugged and huddled against the door again.

"Lock that door, will you? I don't want it springing open and you falling out. I don't have time to go back and pick you up."

A small smile crossed the girl's lips.

"That's better. So who do you think did it, Lily? If it wasn't you, who was it?"

A look of fear sprang up on Lily's face again, but she remained silent.

"So you think it was your father."

Lily nearly jumped out of her seat. "I didn't say that! No, no!"

"Relax, kid. You think your father did it, he thinks you did it, both of you are scared the other one killed the elf."

"Connie, his name was Connie." Her tone was quarrelsome, challenging.

"All right. Connie."

"And I really liked him," she said in a simple, child's voice. "Do you think my father… killed him?"

"He seems to have an airtight alibi, but I don't know yet. When I find out for certain, you'll be the first person I tell. Try to get some sleep. We've got another hour's worth of travel."

Chapter Six

The rain didn't let up and the ride took closer to an hour and a half. Percy pulled up to the corner of second and Houston. She parked in her usual spot, directly across the street from her apartment stoop, and rolled down the fogged up window. Looking around, she saw there was no one out in this downpour, not even the usual venders. Too bad, she would've liked a hotdog about now, about the only meat she saw these days, but this way their entrance into the building was unobserved.

"Hey, wake up, Sleeping Beauty." She tapped Lily on the shoulder.

The girl had dropped off instantly and hadn't stirred once during the trip back to Manhattan's lower east side. Percy hustled the groggy girl out of the car, and up three flights to her family's apartment. Lily was silent the entire time. Percy couldn't figure out if she was still half asleep or shocked to see how the have-nots lived. This time of day the hallways and landings, often filled with children spilling out into them from their apartments, were eerily quiet.

Percy tried the handle and opened the unlocked apartment door, clucking to herself. No matter how many times she and Pop told everyone to be sure to lock up after themselves, they rarely did. She threw the door wide open. It, too, was eerily quiet. She did a mental rundown. Sera, working; Oliver, school; Mother, shopping; Pop no doubt napping. He slept a lot these days.

"Come on in, but try not to drip on anything." she said to Lily in a muted voice. Wordless, Lily followed her inside. "Let's try to keep it down. My father is probably sleeping. Take off your hat and coat and leave them there." Percy pointed to a rack nailed to the wall above an empty umbrella stand.

Lily unbuttoned her coat, removed it along with the hat, while Percy hurriedly took off her wet things, shook them vigorously and threw them on the rack, talking in hushed tones continually.

"This is the place I'm sharing for the time being with my family. That would be my mother, father, son, and God help me, my kid sister, who's a year or two older than you. You'll stay here for now. It ain't the Ritz, but nobody will be looking for you here."

She picked up the suitcase and walked down the long hallway, trailed by a docile Lily. With a cautious glance at the girl, Percy wondered what was going on in her mind.

Exhausted? Shocked? Planning an escape? I need to be ready.

Pointing to doors shooting off to the left and right she said, "That's my office slash bedroom. The parlor is opposite. You'll be in Oliver's room; he'll bunk with me."

Percy pushed open the door of a ten by twelve room, containing a single bed and dresser drawers. A small desk and chair were strewn with comic books. Happy, yellow curtains and a matching bedspread stood out against light blue walls. Posters of different types of World War I and II warplanes were taped or nailed here and there. Three miniature wooden model airplanes swung from the center of the ceiling on strings. All in all, it was a warm and inviting small boy's bedroom.

A smile flickered on Lily's face as she looked around, her first reaction to anything. The older woman dropped the big suitcase next to the dresser and went to the head of the neatly made bed. She reached under the pillow and pulled out her son's green and white striped pajamas then went to the top drawer of the dresser and removed her child's neatly folded underwear.

Lily took a few steps, placed the small overnight case at the foot of the bed and sat heavily on the mattress next to it, feet dangling off the floor. While Lily looked around at her new surroundings, Percy observed her. The detective still wasn't sure about the girl's character, but was relatively sure Lily didn't kill the elf. That's all she cared about.

That and five-thousand buckaroos.

"Bathroom's across the hall," she stated. "Fresh towels in the linen closet – one a week is the allotment. Kitchen is at the end of the hallway." She came and stood in front of Lily. "Here are the rules. You can't leave this apartment and you can't call or write anyone to tell them where you are."

"But my father--" Lily began to protest.

"I'll take care of your father." Lily didn't look convinced. "I mean it, kid, you don't call anyone or go out, and you need to promise me that. You stay inside the apartment, preferably this room, except for meals. And when you finish eating, you clear your plate from the table and you take it to the sink, just like you pick up after yourself in the bathroom. As Mother says, 'it's the maid's day off'. You got me?"

"Yes, I got you." Lily repeated. She looked up at the older woman. "Thank you, Miss Cole." Lily stared at Percy with clear brown eyes, flashing her own acceptance at being odd man out. "You don't like me much, do you?"

"Jury isn't in yet. But I think you've got the perfect name. *'Consider the lilies, how they grow: they neither toil nor spin.'*"

"'*But I tell you, not even Solomon in all his glory clothed himself like one of these.*'" Lily completed the Biblical phrase, her voice ringing out in the small room. She glanced up at Percy.

"My father and I used to go to Sunday School together. That was before my mother died. I can't help it if I'm rich."

"No, I suppose you can't, but try not to flaunt it around here."

Lily flushed and turned away. "I'll try to be as little trouble as possible. What are you going to do now?"

"I'm going to make a few calls, but first I need to ask you a question. This Connie, did he have any enemies?"

Lily shook her head. "Not that I know of. Everyone likes…liked…Connie. But I didn't know him that well."

But you knew him well enough to have sex with him in the middle of a fifth Avenue store window? Whoops! Watch that school marm crap, Percy.

Lily went on, "I only met him at Santa Land a few weeks ago."

"Well, I'll check that place out, too. You hungry?"

Lily nodded, almost ashamed of the admission.

"We don't have much fancy stuff around here, but the icebox has some Spam in it and probably leftover oatmeal. Unless you want some pistachios. I got some here." She reached inside her trouser pocket.

Lily's face lit up. "I love oatmeal. With butter and brown sugar?" She added the request, hopefully.

Percy pulled her empty hand out and shook her head. "We got armored cow, sister. That's canned milk. No butter, no brown sugar. Maybe a little regular sugar. I'll see. Meanwhile, settle in, unpack – use the top drawer of the dresser -- and come on down to the kitchen in about five minutes. We don't do room service here."

Percy shut the door behind her, went to her own room, tossed Oliver's clothes on the bed, towel-dried her damp hair, and headed out to the kitchen. She pushed the door open, expecting the room to be empty and was surprised to see her father sitting in his wheelchair staring out at the rain from the four-paned window. His face looked worried and grim.

Her voice broke the silence. "Pop, what's wrong?"

With a start, the silver-haired man turned to his eldest daughter, a smile crossing his face.

"Persephone, I didn't hear you come in." He turned the wheelchair from the window and wheeled himself across the large room and toward her.

She hurried forward and dropped to her knees, coming eye to eye with her father.

"What is it, Pop? I can tell something bad has happened."

"It's not that much," Pop said in a dismissive manner. He touched her face with gentle fingertips then turned and wheeled himself a few feet away from his daughter. "The doctor was here a while ago and--"

"And what, Pop?"

"He wants to put me back in the hospital. Seems this old leg still isn't healing right." Pop gave out a short bark of a laugh. "I could have told him that."

Percy waited, saying nothing. She knew there was more.

"He might have to take it." While his voice was light, his body sunk into itself in defeat and resignation.

Percy swallowed the scream rising in her throat and said nothing.

Her father went on, "He says I've got an infection in the bone, called Osteomyelitis or something like that." He shrugged. "This old thing's not much good to me now, anyway. I've seen plenty of men get by with one leg." He almost broke down but rallied. "Frankly, I'm glad to lose the leg if it means I lose the pain. Don't tell Mother. I'll tell her when the time is right."

"Pop, isn't there anything? Anything else they can do? There must be something!"

"Well, there's this new stuff called penicillin, and he wishes he could try that. But it costs a fortune."

Percy thought about the two hundred and ninety-five dollars resting in her pocket. "How much?" *Christmas will have to wait.*

Pop smiled and shook his head. "Fifty dollars a shot. Fifty! And he said I'd need at least eight of them. Even then, there's no guarantee."

"But he could try that, right? If it could kill the infection, maybe you could keep your leg, right?"

"Persephone." His voice radiated exasperation and defeat on the single word. "Where am I--"

"Here, Pop," she said standing up. She thrust a hand into her pocket and pulled out the roll of money. "Here's, two hundred and ninety-five bucks. We're a hundred and five bucks short but at least this'll get us started. Maybe he'll float you the rest until I get it. And I'll get it, I swear." She rolled the money up, dropped down and, taking her father's hand, forced it into his palm. She closed his fist and wrapped her hand around his. "Take it, Pop, it's the only way."

If Waller wants any of it back, tough.

"Where'd you get all that money?" Her father's face was clearly astonished. "You didn't do nothing dishonest, did you? The name of Cole has never been--"

"No, no, Pop. All above board." She stood up again. "Mr. Waller, the new client, gave it to me as an advance. It's the dead elf job. That reminds me, Pop, I've got his daughter in Oliver's room."

"The dead elf's daughter?"

"No, no, Pop, Lily Waller, the jeweler's daughter. It was her gun that shot the man, but I don't think she did it. She's going to stay with us for a few days until I find out who killed Connie."

"I thought it was a man who got shot."

"It is. It was. The dead elf's name was Conrad Barnes. They called him Connie."

Pop slammed his hand down on the armrest in frustration. "What is this world coming to, Persephone? People call you, a girl, Percy. Then they call a man Connie. I don't--"

"Pop, Pop, stop." She burst out laughing. After a moment, so did her father. "I think I know why you and Mother have lasted this long." Sobering, she added, "Pop, go call the doctor. Tell him you want to start those shots right away. You got the money now or most of it. Okay? There's no better use for it."

Pop opened his hand and stared at the wad of bills. "I can't take this. Take money like this from one of my children? What have I come to?"

"Come on, Pop. It's only money. That's what it's for."

He searched her face. "Persephone, Persephone, Persephone, you're such a sweet girl, always were. The outside is Norse, like your ancestors, but inside pure angel --" He reached out and tried to fold his arms around her.

"Ah, Pop, stop already." She pretended to fight his affection off. "I love you, too, but don't go all mushy on me."

"Just one little hug, Persephone? What could it hurt?"

"Okay, but you got to take the money, Pop." She gave him a quick hug and broke free. "Okay?" She searched his face.

Pop nodded then looked down. "Okay." He held the bills, looking down at the wad then thrust them into his shirt pocket. "I liked it better, though, when you were my secretary, being safe. Not out there doing investigating, like the killing of an elf. It isn't right; you could get hurt. If only I could get out of this chair…." He stopped speaking and shook his head slowly.

"I want you out of the chair, too, and you will be soon. But *I* like this better, Pop, and that should count for something."

Pop pushed away, still shaking his head. Percy went on.

"Even when you get well, I don't want to go back to being your secretary. I'm a detective now. I even got a license. It's been hanging on the wall for months. Why can't I be your partner, the same as Uncle Gill?"

Pop whirled his wheelchair around to face his daughter. "Gilleathain was my elder brother and a *man*. We were both on the police force before the Depression laid us off. Then he got us the jobs for the meat packing industry down on Fourteenth Street fighting illegal drinking, but we worked our way up and started our own business."

The same old story again and again.

In frustration, Percy rolled her eyes. "Uncle Gill's been gone for two years. Liquor's legal and we got to make a living with the cases that come along. I've been doing this with you side by side, especially after your fall from that catwalk. You remember all the work I did on Macbeth."

"Course I do. I was side by side with you much of the time."

"That's right. I solved the case when nobody else could. And I worked hard to get my PI license. I want a future that means something; I don't want to be a secretary for the rest of my life. Please, Pop."

She watched him study her face for a moment, unsure which way this argument would go. Pop, for all his pleasantness was a man who made up his mind fast, and when he did, few could change it. She sucked in a breath and didn't expel until he spoke.

"Yes, you did solve that case and I've never been prouder. And you worked harder and have been a better partner than pretty near anyone I ever knew." In almost a 180 degree turn, he smacked his hand down on the armrest of the wheelchair. "Things have been changing and we got to go along with the changes." He laughed his warm loud laugh, a

laugh Percy loved since she could remember. "You know, they're talking about taking women on the force? Next they'll be putting them in the fire department."

"And Brinks hired women to be detectives, Pop, last year. Three of them."

"Well, why not? Many's a woman that can hold her own with a man, but especially you, Persephone," he added with pride. "Ninety-five percent of detective work is done in the old noggin," he said, tapping the side of his head. "And you got a better noggin than most."

"Thanks, Pop. Coming from you, that means a lot."

There was a tentative knock on the swinging door.

"That's got to be Lily," Percy said. "Where's Mother, anyway?"

"Picking up a prescription for me at the drugstore." He called out in a louder voice. "Come on in, young lady."

Lilly pushed the door open slowly and stuck her head in. "I'm sorry, I didn't mean --"

"Come on in," Pop repeated, in his usual, genial manner. "We don't stand on ceremony around here."

"Right." Percy crossed her arms and looked at the girl. "There's no need to knock on the kitchen door. Now the bathroom door..."

"Persephone," her father chastised, "As your mother would say, let's not be crude."

Puzzled, Percy looked at him. "That was crude?" She turned back to Lily, who still stood in the doorway, ill at ease. "Sit down, Lily, and I'll get you that oatmeal." Percy moved to the icebox and took out a large bowl covered with a moist cloth.

"We've got some dried apricots left over from last Christmas you can cut up and put on it, if you like," the older man offered.

"Thank you, Mr. Cole, but just the oatmeal." Lily came to the table taking small, hesitant steps.

"And it's not Mr. Cole. It's Pop. Everybody calls me Pop."

"Gee, and here I thought I was the only one that could do that, Pop." Percy grinned and gave her father a wink. She struck a match, lit a burner then took out a large helping of oatmeal and dropped it in a small saucepan. "Lily, if you want milk, there's canned in the icebox. Pop, we got any butter or brown sugar?" He shot her an incredulous look. She, in turn, gave a knowing look to Lily. "Just checking."

"I don't need anything else, really." Lily's reply sounded guilty and tentative.

"Hey, it never hurts to ask, that's my philosophy." Percy went to the pantry, tugged at the overhead pull-chain, and stepped inside. "Aha, just like I thought. Mother's been saving up sugar to make Oliver a birthday cake. I'm sure she won't mind if you have a teaspoon or two." She brought out a jar filled with white sugar and set it next to the stove.

"Thanks." Lily crossed over to the stove. More assertive, she said, "If you want, I can take over."

"You know how to cook?"

"I love to cook. This isn't cooking, anyway, it's reheating. Step aside, you're burning it," she added, giving Percy a slight nudge. Lily lowered the flame and reached for a large spoon.

"You don't have to tell me twice." Percy moved away and turned to her father. "Pop, don't you have a phone call to make?" She went to the back of the wheelchair and began to push it toward the door.

Pop laughed and nodded. "Okay, okay." With almost balletic grace, he swiveled the chair around and hit the swinging door with the back of it, causing the door to open wide. With perfect timing, he wheeled himself into the hallway before the door started to close.

"And, Pop," Percy called out, "Be sure to tell everybody about the new sleeping arrangements when they get home. I've got to run out for awhile."

"Will do, Persephone." His voice reverberated from the hallway.

Percy turned back to Lily, who was still stirring the pot. "So if I'm not needed here, I have to put on some dry clothes and go back to the jewelry store. There are a few things I want to check on." Lily looked over her shoulder and smiled, more relaxed than Percy had seen her. "You really like doing that cooking stuff?"

Lily's smile turned shy but confident. "When I was a child, I wanted to be a pastry chef."

"No kidding?"

"No kidding." Lily returned her attention to the stove. "But father doesn't think ladies should do that sort of thing. So now I'm a lily of the field."

"I shouldn't have said that."

"Why not? It's true."

"It doesn't have to be."

Lily looked up from the stove, in pleasant astonishment. "Thank you for saying that."

"Well, don't get used to me saying nice things. I don't as a rule."

"I'll remember that."

"See that you do."

"You also like to have the last word, don't you?" Lily filled the bowl with the steaming cereal and carried it to the table.

"I do." Percy laughed, as she closed the door behind her.

Chapter Seven

Even with a half a tank of gas in Ophelia, Percy opted to take the subway back to the east side, traffic at this time of day being what it was. Waiting on the platform of the IND, where it was at least warmer, holiday shoppers were out in full force. Many were drawn into the city from Queens, Brooklyn, the Bronx, and New Jersey. Some, like Percy, were Manhattanites, opting for a fast and economical way to get around. With the U.S. entrance into the war, money and presents should have been slim for the gift giving season, but many grinning people carried large parcels, no doubt unexpected presents for under the tree. Persephone Cole and family would not be burdened with unexpected presents this year despite the current windfall.

That's to save Pop's leg. If we can pull that off, present enough.

A man, hardly more than a teenager, was selling Christmas corsages off a big tray hanging in front of him. Dozens of single red roses wrapped in red and green ribbons and decorated with small silver bells lay in rows. A wide canvas strap hung around his neck keeping the tray upright. Each corsage sold for ten-cents apiece, a lot of money for something that would wither and die the next day.

Percy watched him as he walked up and down the platform of the subway station, singing out the glories of his wares, his smile never fading. She was relieved when an elderly lady, her round, pallid face standing out against her all-black clothing and hat, picked through his tray with black-gloved hands. The lady plucked two corsages out, one for herself and one for a little girl standing beside her in a bright blue coat, probably her granddaughter. With a light laugh, the lady bent over and pinned the corsage to the lapel of the girl's coat, eliciting smiles from nearly everyone standing nearby. Just then the train came, and everyone clamored aboard, but Percy's spirits had been lifted. Christmas had a way of doing that.

She arrived at Waller and Son Jewelers just as a happy, youthful couple were exiting, giggles overtaking their attempt at grown-up solemnity.

Love blooms, Percy thought, *even in the dead of winter.*

The dead elf window had been done over, now containing a Lionel train set circling around several sapphire and diamond pendent and earring sets. Tinsel covered red balls hung from pine branches overhead and a nativity set sat in one corner. The window had a hurried, makeshift appearance about it.

She pushed the door open and entered, a tinkling bell giving off an elegant warning. She looked around but saw no evidence of murder and mayhem occurring a few short hours before.

Death happens but life goes on, Toots. Better to keep an updated will at all times.

Behind the counter and paying no mind to the charming tinkling sound overhead, Mr. Waller whispered to a woman, whose age was somewhere between forty-five and fifty. The woman looked as if she couldn't decide if she wanted to be a call girl or a librarian. From the neck down, a tight-fitting, low-cut, short dress emphasized her bosom and
hips.

Well-shaped nylon clad legs wore the latest high-heeled shoes. From the neck up, however, no jewelry or makeup adorned her. Mousy brown hair was pulled back in a bun atop her head so tight Percy couldn't fathom how it didn't hurt. Each hair was as taut as a fiddler's bow string.

Percy's hand flew to her own hair resting at the nape of her neck in a thick, curly ponytail. Unchecked tendrils framed her face in long ringlets. She would never be able to get her hair under control the way this woman did, even if she used all the barreled grease from her cousin's auto repair shop.

With a wry smile, Percy took a moment to size up the man and woman's familiarity and comfort with one another.

Secrets. These two are buried in secrets. I think Waller knows this broad better than any of the diamonds under his loop.

The jeweler finally saw Percy standing in the doorway and his face tensed up, checkered with worry and concern. "Miss Cole, do you have news for me?"

Percy didn't reply, but gestured with her head toward his back office. The woman cleared her throat and looked over the jeweler.

Waller added as an afterthought, "Oh, Janice, this is Miss Cole. Miss Cole, this is my assistant, Janice Lorner." The mouse nodded a curt greeting, then moved to the other end of the counter, bent over, and began to arrange diamond rings inside a case.

"Why don't we go to my office?" Mr. Waller crossed to the hall door and held it open for Percy, who stepped through and continued into the office. She noticed the philodendron was already doing better. Percy turned to face the jeweler close on her heels.

"You daughter is safe," she said, in a quiet voice.

"Is she? Good. I'm relieved. Where is Lily?"

"Let me worry about that."

"But I have a right --"

"No, you don't," Percy interrupted. "That's what you're paying me for. And if the cops ask you where she is, you don't know and it's legit. Got it?"

"All right, but I don't like it."

Percy shrugged, but didn't say anything. "Before I head over to Santa Land, you need to be more forthcoming with me."

"What are you talking about? I --"

"Over the phone you told me you never saw the dead elf before, but when I got here, you said you found him and your daughter at your Long Island place playing hide the salami. Now which is it?" Her eyes narrowed on him, and she waited for him to speak.

He hesitated then took a deep breath. "I only said I'd never seen him before in case the police were listening in. I don't want them to know my daughter had been seeing him and I knew about it."

"You didn't think that one through, mister. They're going to find out he's been out at your little mansion with your kid, you knew it, and because you didn't tell them, they're going to suspect you might have done him in. Sort of like I do."

Waller's face flashed an expression of shock. "I didn't think of that."

"Maybe you didn't, but maybe you did. So now I have to ask you the big question, and don't lie to me. Like I told your daughter, I don't like it."

He said nothing, but nodded in assent.

"You kill Conrad Barnes?" She jumped in quickly before he could speak. "Listen, Waller, if you did I don't care." She stopped talking for a moment, scrutinized his face.

This is a big lie, buster. I do care. But you wouldn't be the first person with money and power to think he was above the law.

Percy went on in a friendly, easy tone. "Even if you did, you've probably got enough dough to get off with a slap on the wrist and you can stop the hunt for Lily. So tell me how it goes. It'll make life easier for all concerned."

"Me? Kill the man?" His face was spotted at first with astonishment then anger. "Why if I killed all the men…who…who…" He stopped speaking, clearly at a loss for words.

"Schtupped your daughter?"

Waller bit back any retort and merely said, "Had relations with my daughter--"

So that's where Lily got the word.

"What you're saying is, and let's be clear about this, you didn't kill the man? Remember, I won't think less of you if you did. I won't even turn you in to the cops. After all, you're my client. But if you did do it, maybe I can help you."

He looked Percy dead in the eye. "No, I did not kill the man. I was afraid..." Waller turned away.

"You were afraid Lily did. And she thinks *you* did." Percy let out a hoot of laughter. "Okay. I get it. You're both on the dumb side, but I get it." She stood. "Mind if I have a few words with your assistant?"

"Miss Lorner? But why--"

"Because. That's why." Percy's voice overrode his on her way out of the office. In the front of the shop, the assistant polished a bracelet before handing it off to an ancient thin man, who cradled the bauble like it was his first grandchild. A uniformed chauffeur, probably the old duffer's, leaned against the doorway, arms crossed, eyes half-closed.

Percy crooked a finger and gestured for Miss Lorner to come over. The uptight mouse looked at the jeweler standing in the doorway, as if for permission. Mr. Waller walked to his assistant's side.

"I'll take over, Miss Lorner."

With murmured apologies to the customer, Miss Lorner strode toward Percy, who noticed she was clad in heels similar to the ones she had seen on Lily's feet.

I'll have to watch myself. I've already been clipped by a pair of those today. Once is enough, already.

Miss Lorner planted herself in front of the Percy as rigid as a pillar. "Yes?" Her voice was deferential on the surface, but underneath colder than the East River in February.

"I have a question for you, Miss Lorner." Percy wore a smile to offset the command. The woman nodded assent but remained unyielding and silent.

Okay, so nice is not the approach with this broad.

Losing the smile, Percy said, "So about Lily Waller, you like her or not?"

"I beg your pardon?" The question clearly threw the woman, but she kept her voice down.

"Strikes me as a simple question. Waller's kid, you can't stand her or what?"

"It's not for me to--" the assistant began to say. She licked dry lips and glanced in the direction of her boss, who was still busy with a customer.

"Don't be looking over at him for an okay on every word you say to me, lady. Keep your eyes on me." The assistant obeyed. "You want to help your man or not? Or did you already help him by plugging his daughter's latest bad choice in men?"

It took a moment for Janice Lorner to understand what Percy was saying, "Why, how dare you imply that I would ever--"

"It's infer," Percy interrupted. "I'm not making a suggestion without being explicit. I'm being very explicit; I'm saying it outright. That makes it an inference."

Miss Lorner glared at her. Percy glared right back.

"You're a real smarty pants, you know that?" The woman finally uttered.

Percy studied the shorter woman for a moment then broke into a genuine smile. "I was called that earlier today. I was pretty sure you and Waller were having *relations*, but now I know for sure. Thanks for the info." Percy turned and headed for the door.

"Wait a minute." Miss Lorner came after Percy. She glanced over her shoulder at the jeweler deep in conversation with the customer who was arguing the finer point of something or other. The assistant forced a tight smile. "I will grant you, Lily and I have had our differences, but I never met her latest boyfriend, if you can call him that."

"You never met him here or at the Long Island house?"

"I've never been out there. William and I…Mr. Waller and I have conducted our --"

"Relations?"

"Ourselves," Miss Lorner said primly, "always here in the city."

"Umm. You never met this elf…ah… dead man?

"No, but I'm sure he was fairly despicable. They usually were."

"Uh-huh. No doubt Lily thinks the same thing about her father's choices." Percy turned and headed for the exit, stopped again by the other woman's voice.

"Ask her about Danny," Miss Lorner said in a louder voice than she'd meant. She gave a hasty look to her employer and the elderly man, but they were paying rapt attention to the bracelet sparkling between them on a piece of black velvet on the countertop. The mouse moved closer to Percy and repeated through clenched teeth. "Ask her about Danny."

Percy nodded, stepped onto the sidewalk and opened her umbrella.

Why I bothered defending the kid to that woman, I'll never know. Maybe I'm starting to feel sorry for Lily. Or maybe I don't like the mouse's hairdo. And who the hell is Danny?

The rain had stopped for the moment. Umbrellas along the crowded sidewalks closed one by one, making it easier to

traverse the cement pathway without getting your eye poked out.

Percy closed her black umbrella, the one with the bent spoke but never otherwise would die, and rounded the corner of 59th street. She looked down the long, congested sidewalk between Fifth and Madison Avenues.

Waller and his jewels resided in a modern but boring sand-colored structure straddling both Fifty-Ninth Street and Fifth Avenue. Set in about fifty feet on Fifty-Ninth, this dull building abutted an older red brick one. Two small side-by-side stores, a watch repair and cobbler, occupied a small section of the ground floor of the brick. Going out of business signs dominated their windows. Percy found that interesting. She looked up and studied the run down six-story building, housing the two about-to-become-ex shops. A doorway stood in the middle, with stairs obviously leading to the five stories above, probably apartments. The above floors showed to be empty with boarded or soaped up windows. Draped between two center windows was a large but weathered banner reading "Harrison Construction. Making a better future for tomorrow today."

Okay, so a rich, corporate SOB is tearing down a perfectly good apartment building to put up another one so they can make more big bucks. I wonder if Waller's store is also taking a dive? I'll have to ask him.

To the right of these two dismal shops was a bigger store, brightly lit, windows pounding Christmas cheer at passersby. With a 'hit the customer over the head' approach, blinking lights directed your attention to large signs silently bellowing "ONLY 7 SHOPPING DAYS 'TIL CHRISTMAS!"

Directly in front of the store, a littered sidewalk held small Christmas trees looking more like the cut off tops of evergreens rather than having been their own trees. To add insult to injury, they were burdened by strands of multicolored lights, threaded haphazardly through delicate branches. Laden down with too much weight and moisture, limbs leaned into themselves and in various directions giving them a downtrodden, sad look. Drenched cardboard cutouts of different sized white stars, red Santas, and brown reindeer hung on clothesline ropes from between the trees, looking more bedraggled than cheery.

Or is this just me? If only it would snow instead of all this rain. Between Pop's leg and the damned rain, I'm feeling as low as the breasts on a sixty-year old flapper.

She paused for a moment and straightened out one of the bent branches of a small tree, while her mind raced. Letting out a deep sigh, she began to chuckle.

Face it, kiddo, what's really bothering you is not being able to afford the red Radio Flyer wagon for Oliver. For a couple of hours with that 300 hundred bucks burning a hole in your pocket, you kept picturing the look on Oliver's face when he unwrapped it on Christmas morning. He asks for so little and he's such a good kid. But Pop's health comes first. Tough choices are just a part of life. You'd better face that one, too, kiddo.

She let out another sigh and headed for the store entrance. Percy tried to concentrate on the case. Sometimes it pays to stop thinking.

When Percy entered the store, she felt smacked in the face by the gaudier side of Christmas. Large and small toys of every description for any aged child, whether stuffed, metal, tin, plastic, moving, or non-moving were heaped on the floor or crammed into row after row of shelving. Near the two entrances and exits of the store, frazzled looking clerks worked long lines at checkout counters.

Percy blinked her eyes several times and looked up. All four walls of the expansive room were covered with Christmas gewgaws. Looped garlands of dried out juniper and pine were stuck between faded wreaths dolloped with limp ribbons and bows in colors of red green, blue, gold, and silver. Chunks of phony greenery and stubby, red holly filled in the remaining empty spots on the walls looking more haphazard than planned. Red and white plastic candy canes, some four feet in length, hung from the ceiling spinning in the air currents and competed for space with large bobbing, silver glittered snowflakes.

Then there was the din. Clicking, clacking, whirling, screeching, sirens, bells, whistles, and voices of small children filled the air. If Percy had been wondering where the kids were with only a week until Christmas, she found them now. Odds were every kid not in school was here, forced to wait inside due to the inclement weather. Two long lines of small children stood - and not so patiently -- next to stunned-looking parents, each waiting for a chance to sit on Santa's lap and put in a last-minute bid for presents.

Percy's gaze followed the antsy kids at the back of the line to the exhausted ones in the front, where a raised platform ran the entire width of the store. More like a movie set, it was someone's idea of what the North Pole might look like in a six-year olds' wildest dreams. It was so overwhelming, you had to focus in on one thing. Percy started at the top and worked her way down.

Fluffy clouds of white cotton hovered overhead in a painted blue sky. On the roof of an actual size Hansel and Gretel style cottage stood several full-scale reindeer. Harnessed to Santa's sleigh, they seemed ready to make a quick getaway at any moment.

I know that's what I'd be planning if I was one of them.

The cottage itself was covered with mammoth pieces of fake but colorful hard candy. A life-size Mrs. Santa Clause marionette stood in the doorway, one hand waving in staccato movements, a clownish smile slathered across her face. No fewer than a dozen four- and five-foot tall snowmen, topped with black satin hats and wearing green or red neck scarves, waved back to Mrs. Clause, apparently seeing her through black coal eyes. From a corner, a one dimensional, silver-foil

Star of Bethlehem beamed down at the end of a stiff wire, giving a modicum of religion to the scene.

In the center of this mess sat Santa's gold-painted throne, complete with red cushions for his little round butt to rest upon, should he be sitting there. But he wasn't. Obviously on a break, a sign in front of the stairs leading to this delightful little scene read, "Back in 15 minutes. I had to go feed my reindeer!"

One small lone elf, looking red-faced, sweaty and tired, tried to control a lynch-mob mentality rising among the waiting throng. This man was a midget instead of a dwarf, his body small but in perfect proportion, but he wore the same getup as Connie Barnes had.

Trying to placate one nearby set of parents was a short, stout woman dressed as an angel, wearing a dingy white gown trimmed in silver. Battered silver wings rested on her shoulders and her head was topped off with a crooked, silver halo. She waved a wand in a menacing manner to an irate parent. As sweaty and red-faced as the elf, her halo bobbed precariously to one side, as she shook her head 'no.'

Percy pushed her way through the raucous crowd and placed herself in front of the harried woman. "Hey, Angel," Percy said in a loud voice, demanding her attention. "Where's the boss?"

"If you mean Santa, he's in the john." The angel's reply came with a snarl. "If you mean the owner of this place, Harry's in his office in the back." She gestured behind her with a poke of the wand. "Sure, why should he be out here paying attention to what's happening?" She grumbled. "Leave it to us!"

"You got that right." The elf, whose fake pointy right ear was coming unglued, nodded. His bitterness was almost palpable. "Two people down and he stays in his office."

"Thanks." Percy picked her way through the horde of kids and heading in the direction of the wand tip. She turned

to the elf. "Better fix your ear, Elfie. Wouldn't want to disillusion the kids."

The little man shot her a big dirty look and went back to policing the crowd. Percy jaunted around the raised platform and found a door in back. She knocked loudly and entered, just as a paunchy man in his mid-fifties said, "Come in."

"You Harry?" Percy stood in the doorway. A small, brown dog roused from his basket, stood, gave a sharp yip, and a quick wag of his tail.

"Quiet, boy," Harry muttered to the dog. The short-legged dog turned around three times, lay down, and resumed his nap. The man swiveled in his desk chair to face Percy, pulled a cigar butt from between his lips, and sneezed.

"Yeah, that's me. Who wants to know?" He pulled a handkerchief from his back pocket and blew his nose. "Damned cold."

"Gesundheit." Percy stepped inside, closing the door behind her before she answered. "My name is Persephone Cole and I'm investigating the murder of one of your employees, Conrad Barnes."

"Oh, Jesus, that! What a time to kill somebody, during my busy season." The man, first annoyed, was now puzzled. "They got gal cops now?"

"I'm not with the New York City Police. I'm a private detective and I want to ask you some questions."

"A private dick, huh?" His leering eyes seemed to appraise her as they went from her black booted feet to the top of her red hair. "A female private dick." He let out a chuckle, eyes resting on her bosom.

"Eyes on my face, Harry." He reluctantly complied. "I'm working for the Waller family. You know, Lily Waller, one of your other elves."

"That stupid girl had to go and shoot him, right in the—"

"Yeah, yeah, I know. Right in the middle of your busy season," she interrupted. "What do you know about Connie Barnes?"

"Why should I tell you anything?" He stuck the cigar butt in his mouth and swiveled back to face a desk laden with papers and small Christmas objects. The dog let out a snort, but slept on.

Percy strode over, grabbed his chair by the armrests, and swung it around to face her. His eyes were even with her breasts, which he leered at again. She grabbed his chin and pushed it up to her face.

"Pay attention to what I'm going to say, Harry. This could save you a lot of trouble. Here's the deal. I happen to have a few cop friends at the precinct, who owe me favors. Now I can see you don't have quite enough exits for as many kids waiting to see Santa, should there be a fire." These sorts of lies came easily to her. "I would hate for you to get closed down, especially in the middle of your busy season."

"The cops were here earlier," he sputtered. "They didn't say anything."

"They don't count as good as me. But I know the law and you're an exit short, should I bring it to their attention."

"All right, all right, save the strong arm tactics. I got his file somewhere in that drawer." He pointed to a dinged wooden file cabinet.

Percy made a move to where he indicated.

"It's private, you know," he added, with more pomp than truth. "You can't go rifling around in there."

"Then you do it for me, Harry." Percy laced her reply with mock sweetness. "Get me the Barnes file. I'll give it a once over and be on my way."

He let out a deep sigh then rose. The dog didn't stir. Percy took a step back and let the balding man pass in front of her on his way to the corner cabinet. Pulling the drawer open

with annoyance, Harry moved practiced fingers through files until he came to the one he wanted.

"Give me Lily's while you're in there," Percy ordered.

Harry thought for a moment, shrugged, and pilfered through the drawer for the file. He drew it out, started to hand both over to her outstretched fingers then pulled back, clasping the files to his chest.

His face broke into a broad grin, as he waggled his eyebrows. "What are you doing later tonight? I think you and I could make beautiful music together."

"I'm tone deaf, Harry. Hand the files over." She stretched out her hand again. "Besides, what would Mrs. Harry say?"

Harry looked surprised. "How did you know I had a wife?"

"There's always a Mrs. Harry, Harry. And if you don't want people to know you've got a family, lose the picture on your desk. Now give." She gestured to the files and snapped her fingers.

He handed them over, went back to his desk, and turned the picture of his wife, teenage son, and himself - back in the days when he had a full head of hair -- on its face. Then he reached down and stroked the sleeping dog while Percy opened Lily's file.

Surprised to see it only contained two pieces of paper, an application for the job and a W2 form, Percy moved to a corner of the room for more privacy. Still standing, she silently read the application. Not much information Percy didn't know, other than Lily listing the Sands Point librarian, Miss Ethel Hornblatt, as one of her two references.

This might explain the suitcase full of books I humped up the stairs. So she's a reader and a cook. There might be more to this kid than I thought.

Percy glanced at the name of the other reference, a society blueblood, Cynthia Van Patterson. Percy read about

Van Patterson's 'youthful exuberance' from time to time, mostly for getting herself arrested. The last time her escapades appeared in the papers, she'd beaned the head waiter of Twenty-One with her umbrella, sent him to the hospital, and paid the man the healthy sum of ten thousand dollars to avoid him pressing charges.

So much for there being more to the kid than I thought.

Percy closed the girl's file with disgust, half at herself for making Lily guilty by association, half at a class of people who could pay for their sins with greenbacks. She flipped it open again, and read the girl's W2 form. Lily had never been employed and listed herself as a dependent of her father.

Percy moved on to Conrad's file. It, too, only contained two pieces of paper, with not much written on either. Obviously, Harry wasn't that concerned about the kind of person who filled his seasonal jobs. Or maybe he was that way about all his employees.

Come to think of it, most employers wouldn't hire those two bozos out front, with or without their costumes.

She read the W2 form and was shocked.

Four dependents? So this Romeo was married. Margaret Barnes, wife. Well, she's a widow now. Living in Manhattan with two kids. I wonder if Lily knows he was married?

Percy read on.

Interesting. He was at Barnes Manufacturing for twelve years before here. Wait a minute. The same name as his? Hmmm.

She turned to the application, which was blank except for his home address.

He lived at the Dakota? That fancy schmancy place over on the west side? You got to buy there, they don't rent. Holy Cow, maybe this guy had money, too, just like our Lily. Well, why not? You can be short and rich; no law says you can't.

She looked up and studied Harry's broad back as he bent over a stack of papers. Either he was deliberately ignoring her or lost in his work. Her face took on a scowl.

What the hell was Connie doing working as an elf here? Maybe the same thing as Lily, a lark. Crap, if I had money, my lark would be to winter in Florida, not work for a scumbag like Harry.

Percy took out a notepad from her pants pocket, made some notes then threw the files on the desk in front of Harry, who jerked his head up.

"You done? Not much to read," he said.

"Done. Thanks." The dog opened its eyes at the sound of her voice but didn't move. "One more thing, you got lockers somewhere for the employees to stash their stuff?"

"You kidding? They get dressed in the bathrooms. That's good enough."

"So there's nothing left around here of either Barnes or Waller?"

"Naw," he said, shaking his head. "The cops asked the same thing. I don't like anybody leaving anything. I'm just here for two months, anyway, from Halloween on. This isn't my regular place. I won't be here next year. They're tearing this building down."

"Where would that be, your regular place?"

"Thirty-fourth and ninth. All those toys out there? I manufacture most of them. This is my big season. So listen, Percival --" he said, turning to her with a toothy smile.

"It's Persephone," she interrupted. "But you can call me Miss Cole. What's the name of your manufacturing company?"

"Barnes and Weinblatt Toys. I'm Weinblatt."

"Barnes. Same name as your dead elf."

"Yeah, his father was my partner way back when."

"When what?"

"When he was alive."

"That would be the father, not the son." Harry stared at her. "Just keeping things clear, Harry. You're talking about the senior Barnes being dead."

"Well," Harry answered with a smile. "They're both dead now."

"True enough." Her returning smile was genuine. "But I like clarification, so continue to clarify."

"Before my partner died, he got out of the toy business and into real estate. Made a bundle. I kept his name; too cheap to redo the signs, I guess. Connie liked to come here since he was a kid and dress up for Christmas."

"You don't sound too broken up about someone you knew since he was a kid."

He shrugged and blew his nose again. "He was strange, even then. I guess being three feet tall does something to a person. You sure you don't want to go out for a beer later tonight? You're just my kind of gal."

"No, I'm not." She headed for the door. "But thanks, Harry. Give my best to your wife and Merry Christmas."

"I don't do Christmas. I've got a bad cold, I'm two elves down, and it's still a week to go," he griped. "I had to promise two days off with pay to that Gertrude bitch to wear an angel costume I found in the basement and then she goes and gets it dirty. She's my bookkeeper."

"Why not an elf? She's short enough."

"No costume. And those bastards took theirs with them last night. I'm going to deduct the cost from their last paychecks. You see if I don't."

"I never doubted it for a minute, Harry," she said, closing the door behind her.

<h1 style="text-align:center">Chapter Eight</h1>

Percy beat her way through the sweaty crowd and exited into a gray sky that was fighting to turn blue. Gloomy clouds still predominated but here and there a patch of sunshine peeked through with a little promise. The weather was a tad warmer, too, hovering somewhere in the mid-forties. But the sun was about to go down in about another 30-minutes.

So enjoy the weather while you can.

A pasty-looking, rotund elderly man, not too steady on his feet, exited the watch repair shop and headed for the curb. He was followed by a small animal.

Jeesh, is that a dog? Looks like an overweight rat.

She watched the dog run over to a parking meter and lift his leg. She turned to the man. "Hi there, Mister. What kind of dog is that?"

The man looked down with fatherly pride at the small brown dog with the lifted leg pouring a steady stream of urine on the base of the meter. He turned back to Percy with a certain amount of disdain. "Haven't you seen one of these before?" Percy shook her head. "It's a Chihuahua. They're from Mexico. You've heard of Xavier Cougat?"

"Sure. Spanish orchestra leader. Isn't he over at the Waldorf?" She could tell this knowledge raised her up a notch or two in the elderly man opinion.

"That he is, young lady. One of the most talented musicians in the world." He made that statement with pride, too. "This is one of his dogs. Not actually his, but one of the dogs bred by the same dog he bought. Or one of them."

I don't know what the hell you just said, Mister, but let's move on from the four-footed.

"This your store?" She pointed to the watch shop.

"That it is. Thirty-two years I've been here repairing watches and clocks. Have to leave by the end of January. Thirty-two years."

"That's too bad. Where are you going to go?"

Before the man could answer, another man several years younger exited the shoe store and walked over with a big smile on his face. He was bundled up as if it were fifteen degrees outside. He looked down at the dog.

"Cougat, boy! Come here, Cougat." The man slapped open palms on his thighs in an effort to get the dog to go to him. Finished with his business, Cougat the dog ran over with a wagging tail and lay down belly up at the man's feet.

That's a pretty obscene position.

"Cougat's certainly a cute little dog," she said to both the men, having no more problem with this lie than the one she gave to Harry about the exits.

The bundled-up man reached down and stroked the dog's exposed, tubby belly. "I like to think I am a second father to Cougat," he said, speaking in a heavy accent, possibly German.

"That you are, Mr. Zimmer, that you are," said the dog owner.

"Thank you, Mr. Pierce," said the other man, straightening up. "Have you seen Earnest today? He promised he would clear out the alley. I still cannot get out the back door."

Mr. Pierce shook his head with a clucking sound. "Ah, these workers. It is not the same as in my day." Both men shared a common look of disapproval then turned to Percy.

She smiled and raised her eyebrows and shrugged in a 'what can you do?' gesture.

Satisfied, Mr. Pierce turned back to the cobbler. "If I see him, I'll tell him you're looking for him, my friend."

"So, Mr. Zimmer, is that your shoe repair? I'm Persephone Cole and I'm investigating the death of Conrad Barnes." She offered her hand to each of the men and they shook it in an automatic but absent-minded manner.

"That was so unexpected." Mr. Zimmer was the first to put his feelings into words. He picked up the dog and cuddled it to his bosom.

"It was indeed, Mr. Zimmer, it was indeed." Mr. Pierce retrieved his dog from the other and began his own cuddling routine while he spoke. "On top of closing down our businesses, now there's a murder! Not a very Merry Christmas."

"Holidays are not always happy." Mr. Zimmer's mood was dark and ominous. "Look at what is going on in Europe." All his 'w's were pronounced as a 'v' and he had heavy rolling r's.

"You're from Germany, Mr. Zimmer?" Persephone asked the man that looked like the weight of the world was on his shoulders.

"Poland. You investigate this murder of the man who was the elf? Is that not what the police are for?"

"I'm a private detective. I've been hired by the family." Each man seemed to accept this explanation. "Did either of you know Mr. Barnes? Or a young lady who also worked at Santa Land, Lily Waller?"

They looked at one another as if for reaffirmation then shook their heads in unison.

"I know nothing, Miss Cole," said Mr. Zimmer. "But it is cold out here and I must get back to my work. Before I close shop there are many shoes to repair." He turned to leave but was stopped by Percy's voice.

"Where will you go from here?"

He hesitated, as if verbalizing the future gave it more sorrow than he might be able to bear. "I look for property nearby but everything is expensive. The lease here was good, a fair lease. Maybe I will have to set up shop in Brooklyn. It is not the same but I will do what I have to do." He turned his back on the two and returned to his store. Both man, woman, and dog watched him enter the building.

"It is so sad," murmured Mr. Pierce. "I am old; I will retire. I don't care that much, but Mr. Zimmer is different. He's only in his forties with only part of his family here. There are many more he's trying to get out of Poland. This is no time for him to lose his business. The worst part for me is cleaning thirty-two years of storage out of the basement. I haven't been down there in years."

"Thanks for your help, Mr. Pierce. I hope you and Cougat enjoy retirement." Percy chucked the little dog under the chin. He growled. She withdrew her hand. "Feisty little guy."

"He is, indeed."

"Okay, so maybe I'll see you around."

"A pleasure, Miss Cole."

Percy, deep in thought, watched the tubby old man carry the tubby little dog into the building.

Chapter Nine

"Who does that bitch detective think she is snooping around here?" He turned away from the dog and ripped open a box, clawing through the contents. "Dolls! Nothing but children's dolls! It's got to be here. I saw it…when?" He froze in place thinking, hands shaking with cold, anger, and fatigue. He shook his head. "So long ago. I can't remember. But I know I saw it…" He exhaled a rheumy breath. "It was nineteen thirty-four? Or was it thirty-five? Why didn't I pay attention?"

He tossed the useless box across the room. It collided with several others. He added the dolls, stiff with age and years of dust, to the ever growing pile in a corner of the musty, cold basement.

"I'll blow her up, too if she gets in my way. Fat bitch detective. I'll fix you, too. I'll fix them all."

Chapter Ten

Percy slipped the nickel in the payphone, closed the door of the booth, and listened for a dial tone. She dialed her home number and waited for someone to pick up the phone.

"Hello," said a small voice, after the fourth ring.

"Just the young man I wanted to talk to," Percy said, a flood of warmth spread through her. "It's mommy, sweetie."

"Mommy!" Oliver went on in a rush. "Guess what we're having for dinner?" The eight-year old didn't wait for an answer. "Pot roast! Pot roast and mashed potatoes and string beans." He took a breath but spoke again before Percy could answer. "And Lily's making an apple pie for dessert! With whipped cream!"

Astonished but pleased, Percy laughed. "That's wonderful, sweetie."

"When you coming home, Mommy?"

"Soon. I have to run over to the west side and talk to a lady first then I'll be home. Did Grandpa tell you you're bunking with me for a few days? Just until we sort a few things out with Lily."

"Sure. I like Lily. She's a lot like Aunt Sera only prettier."

"Don't tell your Aunt Sera that. Did you do your homework?" He made a dejected sound over the phone. "What's wrong?"

"Multiplication tables. I hate them."

"What's twelve times six?" She said, trying to make a game of it.

"We didn't get to the twelve tables yet."

"Okay, what's six times twelve?"

"Oh! That's easy. Seventy-two," he answered.

"Very good. That's six times twelve. Twelve times six is the same answer. All you have to do is reverse it. By the time you get to the twelve tables, you'll know them."

"Wow! Thanks, Mommy."

"Go get your grandpa for me and then finish your homework. I'll see you soon, okay, sweetie?"

She waited for Pop to come on the line and gazed out the glass of the phone booth door, watching people order their evening meals at the drugstore counter. She could have used something to eat herself. It was a long time since the spam sandwich.

She heard her father's voice. "How's everything going, Pop?"

"Couldn't be better. Lily insisted on ordering up groceries and she had ration coupons for stuff like meat, fresh milk, eggs, and butter. It cost sixty-seven dollars, too."

Percy became anxious. "She didn't show herself to the deliveryman did she? I don't want--"

"Of course not. She gave me the money and I paid him off at the door. She says as long as she's here, we're going to eat like kings. She insists on cooking the meals, too. That don't please Mother too much, but she's going along with it. Of course, the boy, Sera, and I are pleased as punch, your mother not being the best cook we know."

"Good, good," Percy answered, anxious to get to the next reason she called and not wanting to run out of her nickel's worth.

"Pop, I need you to get some information for me. You still got that friend at the census bureau?"

"Renaldi? The census bureau? What for?"

"I'll tell you later."She looked at her watch. "But it's nearly five o'clock and I want you to catch him before he leaves for the day. Ask him who's listed as the owner of the building at Sixty-Four east Fifty-Ninth Street, the names of the people who lived there until they got booted out, and what businesses have leases there. Maybe he can write you out a list."

"Census, huh? How far back should I ask Renaldi to go?"

"Hmmm," she thought. "I don't know. Nineteen-thirty, maybe. I'm also interested in finding out who recently bought the building, but that's another department. Harrison Construction is going to be handling the demolition, if that's any help. Maybe you can make a call to some of your cop friends on that one."

"What for, Persephone? Does this have anything to do with the dead elf?"

"I'm not sure, Pop, but whenever there's a change as big as what's going on there, I want to know the particulars. While you're at it, find out about Barnes and Weinblatt Toys, over at thirty-fourth and ninth. This Harry Weinblatt is quite a character."

"You've been a busy girl."

"About to get busier. Don't tell Lily this, but it seems Connie had a wife and a couple of kids. I'm about to pay a visit to the grieving widow."

"Stay dry, Persephone, and we'll save you some grub."

"You're giving me something to look forward to, Pop."

* * * *

A short ride on the cross town bus and Percy legged it up to seventy-second street and Central Park West. It was sprinkling again, and she was glad she had the umbrella, even with its twisted spoke.

She entered the lobby of the Dakota, grand, elegant, and old world. The doorman, a barrel-chested man with a handlebar mustache, gave Percy the once over and was pretty iffy about what he saw. She asked for Mrs. Conrad Barnes and his mustache began to twitch.

"She's got company." His manner was nervous but gruff.

"That's right," Percy lied, "And they're expecting me."

His jaw dropped and he stared at her wide-eyed. "They is? Then you go right up, missy, and good luck to you." He shook his head and turned away.

"Where am I going?"

"14B," He said, sitting behind the desk and snatching up his racing times. "Damned shame, the way some people behave, him not cold in his grave."

What the hell is that all about?

The elevator, almost bigger than her son's room, stopped with a jerk at the fourteenth floor. She heard the music of Guy Lombardo from somewhere down the hall. The closer she got to the apartment door, the louder it got, drowned out by an occasional burst of laughter, sometimes from a man, sometimes from a woman.

Sounds like someone's having a helluva party. Maybe I should have worn my dancing shoes.

As she walked down the hall, her first thought was how the sound could travel so far in such a well-made, sturdy building. When she arrived at the door marked 14B, she discovered the source of the music and that the door had been propped open with several stacked books. A small dog, this time she knew the breed – a wire-haired terrier — came running from somewhere further up the hallway. It looked at her, jumped over the books, and back into the apartment. There, it did a fast turnaround and began to bark insistently; the sound reverberating in Percy's ears, despite lavish rugs and padded furniture.

"Shush, Toby," said a female voice. The dog barked on, while Percy covered her ears to protect them from the piercing noise.

"Toby! Stop that." A needle skidded across a record, as if it had been struck from the side. Guy Lombardo and his band of renown were silenced, but the dog continued to bark.

"Shut up, you fleabag," said the man's voice. "Before I throw something at you."

"Now, Greg, there's no need to get physical." Greg laughed and apparently got physical with the woman, who began to giggle. The dog continued to bark.

Percy rapped on the door with loud, persistent knuckles for a moment or two before she was heard.

"Someone at the door," the woman said to the man. "Who is it?" Her voice was louder and there were sounds of movement to the door and the scooping up of the dog. The door flew open and a dyed redhead with mussed hair, maybe five foot eight or nine and in her mid-thirties, stood before Percy. The woman was barefoot but wearing a short evening dress of royal blue, trimmed with sparkling beads at the neckline.

The dog stopped barking and struggled to be free from her grasp.

"Yes?" She set the dog down, whose job apparently done, scampered away.

"Mrs. Barnes?" *Boy, if you are, being a shrimp didn't cramp the little guy's style.*

"Yes. Who are you? What do you want?"

"My name is Persephone Cole."

"Perse…Per…what Cole?" She focused on Percy with a vacant, bored stare.

Jesus, what a dummy. "Miss Cole will do. I'd like to offer my condolences over the loss of your husband." *That was hard to say with a straight face.*

The woman's demeanor changed and she struck a remorseful pose. "Thank you." Then she dropped the act. "So, what do you want?"

"I wondered if I could speak with you for a few moments. I'm doing some investigative work on behalf of Lily Waller. Did you know her or have ever met her?"

"Hey," said a male voice, obviously standing behind the half-closed door and listening in. "Isn't that the broad that killed Connie?"

The door opened wider and a coatless Greg, wrinkled white shirt half unbuttoned, stepped in front of the barefoot woman, not so much in a protective manner as a possessive one.

From behind his shoulder, Margaret Barnes blurted out, "I never met any of Connie's *friends*. I hadn't even seen the guy in six months."

"Okay, lady," Greg said. His voice and body language took on a belligerent edge. "You got your answer. So take a hike." Fingers holding a cigarette and a hand wrapped around a rock glass filled with amber-colored liquid, he gestured to the processed red-head. Said woman stepped to the side of the tall, rumpled man and leaned her head on his shoulder, staring at Percy with a smirk. "Don't you know we've got a grieving widow here?"

"So it would seem." Percy turned around to leave. "Sorry to have bothered you."

She headed for the elevator at the end of the long hallway. Right before the elevator came, she heard Guy Lombardo's music resume.

* * * *

"Can I ask you a couple of questions, old-timer?"

Percy exited the elevator and strode over to the uniformed man behind the counter, who was still reading the racing form. She took a five-dollar bill out of her pocket, the last of her savings, and set it on the marble-topped counter. "For a fin, maybe you'll tell me what you know about Mrs. Barnes."

He looked up in surprise and his handlebar mustache twitched again. "You back already? Thought they invited you to the party. They're celebrating." He glanced at the fin. "What do you want to know? She's pretty much an open book. She don't care what people see, that one."

"First, where are the kids?"

"Where they usually are, with her mother in Queens. They're normal, those kids. Not like Barnes was." He reached for the money. Her hand was quicker and covered the bill.

"What else?"

"Let's see. Her friend's name is Mr. Gregory Rhodes. He's a dentist. He's been visiting here for about a year."

"I'll bet her teeth have never been cleaner. And Mr. Barnes didn't mind? That's pretty liberal thinking."

"He hasn't lived here for four or five years. I think they have one of those legal separations. At least, that's what I heard the cops say when they was here earlier. I never heard of such a thing. Either you're married or you're not. She gets everything, that wife. I heard that, too."

Percy looked over his shoulder to a newspaper lying on a stool beside the man. "Can I see that paper?"

"This one?" He reached for it. "Sure. You can have it but it's gonna cost you a five-spot."

"It's yours," Percy said with a grin and slid the money to him.

On the front page was the same photo Percy had seen of Lily on her father's desk. She read the large-type heading, 'Have you seen this woman? Lily Waller is wanted for questioning in the murder of Conrad Barnes.'

Percy left the Dakota absorbing every word the New York Globe had to say about her client's daughter. It wasn't pretty.

Chapter Eleven

The door slammed overhead on the ground floor, and he strained his ears for the sounds of the lock being turned. Once he heard it, he closed his magazine, threw off the blanket he'd wrapped around himself, stood up from the bench, and stretched.

"That should be the last of them." He looked around the dim, dank room, his preferred place to stay when down in the basement. The large furnace chugged away making the constant hollow, sucking sound, as it consumed its recent bellyful of coal. His back hurt from the relentless filling of it and he rubbed the back of his neck. In the summer, this room was too hot to be in for very long, not that he couldn't endure it. He could endure anything. But in the winter the heat was a welcome respite from the rest of the damp and cold block-long basement, separated by winding tunnels and locked doors.

"Too many rooms down here. Too many places it could be," he muttered. "Too many. And too many nosy people snooping around in my business."

He picked up a crowbar and headed for the next unexplored tunnel.

Chapter Twelve

Percy heard the hubbub from the kitchen as soon as she opened the apartment door. It made her smile. She felt the warmth of the air then took in the aroma of home cooking.

Be it ever so humble.

Exhaustion enveloped her. It had been a long one. Percy felt like she'd covered the east and west sides of Manhattan on foot. She'd trudged through on and off heavy rain for the past hour, having made the decision not to wait for the cross town bus but to hoof it, saving a nickel. Big mistake. Drenched and chilled, she fought back a sneeze.

I don't want to get a winter cold like good, old Harry has, but like Christmas, 'tis the season.

Rather than heading to the joviality of the kitchen, Percy slipped into the peace of her bedroom. She changed clothes and put on the warm, sheepskin slippers she'd received the previous year for Christmas. She was wearing them out. With any luck, a new pair would show up under the tree in a few days. That was Sera's usual Christmas gift.

While towel-drying her hair, she checked for any written messages Pop might have left on her desk. This was their usual method of communication when one of them was out for the day and the other was manning the office. It had been a long time since Pop was the one out; these days it was her.

No note. Either Pop hadn't reached his friend at the Census Bureau or there was nothing to say. She lay down on the bed, giving in momentarily to the fatigue.

Jeesh, what a day. I've walked my dogs off and got nothing much to show for it, except a newspaper that cost me my last five bucks. Get up, girl. Can't lollygag around just yet.

Percy sat up and looked around. The bedroom she'd known since childhood was a well-worn combination of floral and plaid, in shades of dark green and pale blue, decorated when she was eleven. Only once had she known any other home and that was when she was married for a short time to Leo, the Louse.

She scanned the room filled with memories, mostly good, and tried to give it the jaundiced eye of a stranger. Cramped. She hadn't thought of it being cramped growing up, and maybe it only seemed so now because it was currently doing double duty as her office. For the next few days, it would also contain a small boy, but the thought made her smile. Two toy airplanes sat on the foot of the bed and Oliver's homework was laid out on a corner of her desk. She looked at her son's neat but childlike penmanship.

What a smart boy he is. He was worth everything I went through to keep him. And more. I hope his father doesn't reappear one of these days the way he disappeared, without warning.

She felt a lurch in the pit of her stomach. Eight years he'd been gone, right before Oliver was born, his leaving prompted by the announcement of her pregnancy. She'd never filed for divorce; surely Leo had. Jude kept encouraging her to file but she'd always had better things to do with her money. Particularly, as she'd never heard boo from him in all these years.

Still and all…

Percy pushed the thought of her louse of a husband out of her mind and started for the kitchen with two intentions.

Have some food and find out who this Danny is.

On the other side of the kitchen door, she heard such happiness and camaraderie going on, it gave her pause to interrupt it. Conversation and mirth were infused with the sounds of holiday music on the radio and the occasional clatter of dishes, pots, and pans. As exhausted as she was, it lifted her spirits.

Opening the door, Percy took it all in. Mother was washing dishes but had her head thrown back in outright laughter, something Percy rarely saw her do. Pop and Oliver were playing checkers at one end of the table, while Sera and Lily's heads leaned into one another, one blond, one brunette, deep in conversation about the merits of the red polish on their fingernails. Everyone was giggling or gabbing in a light-hearted, familial way. The heavenly smells of pot roast and mashed potatoes wafted toward her. Percy was so hungry, her stomach grumbled.

Oliver was the first to notice her standing in the doorway. "Mommy!"

Her son jumped up from the table, nearly upsetting the game, and rushed over. Pop laughed and waved. Both girls looked up and smiled their greetings, seemingly already fast friends.

Norman Rockwell step aside, Percy thought. *Meet the Coles.*

Oliver gave her a quick hug, but when she bent down to return it, he tugged on her hand.

"Come on, Mommy, we saved you some dinner. It's in the oven." He rattled on. "Tomorrow Lily says she's going to get us a Christmas tree that goes all the way up to the ceiling." He dragged her over to the stove.

"Now Oliver, you know Santa brings us the tree on Christmas eve along with your presents! We don't want to hurt his feelings, do we?" Oliver shook his head 'no' as she bent down. Percy grabbed her son in a bear hug then turned to Lily. "But thanks, anyway. I mean it."

Embarrassed, Lily smiled and began to move around the salt and pepper shakers, using up what looked like nervous energy.

Mother folded the dishtowel, set it down and joined her daughter and grandson by the stove.

"Hello, Persephone, my dear child," she said after planting a kiss on Percy's cheek. Stunned by the display, Percy gave her a faint smile. Mother went on, "You look tired. You go sit down now. Our sweet Lily, and her name is not Lillian as I first suspected but really, truly Lily, has made a delicious dinner for us this evening and we've saved you some."

"Oh, Mrs. Cole, it was nothing," Lily protested from the table, waving the compliment away.

"Oh, yes it was," Sera replied before Mother could say another word. "It was simply the most delish meal I ever ate."

Percy watched Mother think for a moment then say, "Oh, dear. And here I thought I've made a decent meal or two…"

"Oh, sure, Mother, 'decent' but this was actually good," Sera interrupted.

"Serendipity, you apologize to your mother for being so rude." Pop's tone was harsher than usual. "She's had to make do with sparse ingredients and still turns out many a fine meal." He looked at his wife with a wide smile.

"Why, thank you, Father. I'm certain Lily could give me a lesson or two, though."

"Oh no, Mrs. Cole," Lily offered in a quick, deferential manner. "I'm sure I could learn many things about cooking from *you*."

"Could you, my dear?" Mother thought again. "Well, I am known throughout the neighborhood for my split pea soup." With that, Mother turned away, picked up a potholder, bent down, and opened the oven door.

Simultaneously, Percy and Pop, sitting on opposite sides of Sera, took the opportunity to smack her on each side of her head when Mother wasn't looking. Oliver and Lily bit back laughter.

"Ow!" Sera stuck her tongue out at Percy but turned and smiled apologetically at her father. "Sorry, Pop." She turned around in her chair to her mother. "I'm sorry, Mother. I got carried away. And I just love your split pea soup," she said, crossing her eyes and making a face.

Pop shot her a warning glance. Sera got up from the chair so fast she almost knocked it over. "Why don't I go into the parlor and listen to Our Gal Sal there? Want to come, Lily?"

"No, no," Percy said with haste before Lily could reply. "I need to talk to Lily while I eat."

"Okee-dokey." Sera kicked the door open with her foot and dashed out of the kitchen.

"And don't kick the door, Serendipity," Pop said to himself after she left, with a resigned sigh. He turned to his grandson. "I've been telling her that for years for all the good it does me."

With a glance toward his eldest daughter, he said, "Oliver, why don't you and I join your aunt in the parlor and continue playing checkers?" He winked at Percy, folded the board in two, and began gathering up the checker pieces. "The Green Lantern comes on after Our Gal Sal. Maybe your mother will let us listen to that together, even though it's on past your bedtime."

Oliver's face lit up and he looked at his mother, who nodded approval.

"Just this once, Oliver," Percy said. "A special treat. Then go straight to bed. I'll come and tuck you in later." She watched her son push Pop's wheelchair out the door and turn back with a wave. Mother put a plate laden with food on the table.

"You watch out for this dish, Persephone," her mother said. "It's straight from the oven and very hot."

"I will, Mother, and thanks. I'll wash up and finish drying the dishes when I'm done. Why don't you join everybody else in the parlor?"

Mother nodded and removed her apron, taking in the thinly veiled order with a smile. Both Percy and Lily watched her leave.

Lily was the first to speak. "I'm sorry about the tree, Miss Cole. I didn't mean --"

Percy waved it away. "That's quite all right. We have our traditions, just like everyone else, I imagine."

"We never did. Everything stopped when my mother died. Father was always away on a lot of trips buying diamonds and grandfather was...he was...." Her face hardened. She looked over at Percy, anticipating a remark. "Never mind. I know. Poor little rich girl."

"Doesn't sound like you had much of a family life."

"You have no idea."

Percy studied Lily for a moment. There was more to this subject, but Percy decided to let it ride. She sat down and took a large mouthful of mashed potatoes oozing with butter.

"Mmmmm. I haven't had this much butter in almost a year." She took an appreciative bite of the roast, which came apart at the fork's least insistence. She lifted a second forkful and looked at Lily, who had become quiet and withdrawn.

Nervous, very nervous. Or guilty about something? I'm sure it ain't about the Christmas tree.

"You know Connie was married, Lily?"

A grim look overtook the nervous tic on Lily's young and unmade-up face. "He was legally separated. Maggie started fooling around practically the day after they got married. The only reason Connie didn't get a divorce was because she said she'd drag the kids into court if he filed. He didn't want to hurt them. As long as he sent her money every month, she lived her life and he lived his."

"How civilized. So, Lily, another question. Who's Danny?" Percy watched for the girl's reaction with sharp eyes. If she'd been looking for a strong response, she wasn't to be disappointed.

Chapter Thirteen

A quick intake of breath, a knocked over glass of water, followed by a not so fast recovery, said more than a volume of words. Although Lily tried to keep her body language casual as she mopped up the spilled water, when she finally spoke, her voice was high pitched and shaky. "Danny? You mean Danny Deluca?"

"Apparently, I do."

"Danny doesn't have a thing to do with any of this, not Danny. I mean, what about him? Is he back? He can't be back!" She buried her face in her hands, similar to the way she had at the Long Island mansion.

"Where'd he go?"

"He's at Riker's Island awaiting trial." Lily mumbled. "He's been there since last spring."

"What'd he do?"

Highly agitated, Lily rose from the table, wringing her hands and shaking her head.

"I don't want to talk about it."

"Too bad. What'd he do?"

"He can't be mixed up in this. He can't be. He's in jail on Rikers Island. Unless he got out. Oh, my God! Did he get out?" Lily dropped back in the chair, but didn't say any more.

"Don't make me keep repeating myself. What'd he do to wind up at Rikers, this Danny Deluca?"

Lily wriggled in the chair as if she was sitting in a hot seat. When Lily saw Percy open her mouth to speak again, the girl leapt in with hurried words. "It happened the last time we were out together. Danny was wild, I knew that, but I didn't think…"

Lily's speech slowed then came to a halt. Percy leaned over with her fork and poked the girl on the arm. Lily looked over with a start.

"I eat and you talk," Percy warned, shaking the fork in the girl's face.

"All right, all right." Lily rubbed her arm. "It's just so awful."

"I can handle awful."

"That night Danny… he…I was sitting in my car waiting for him to come out of this liquor store. I didn't know what he was really doing in there. He *said* he was going in for a bottle of whiskey. He asked me to wait in the car; I was still underage. When I heard shots, I looked up and saw him through the plate glass window. He was holding a gun and this little old man fell to the floor." Her face contorted at the memory. "Then I watched Danny open the cash register and clean out the drawer. I couldn't believe it. I…I panicked. I floored the accelerator and drove away. I could hear Danny shouting after me but I didn't stop; I didn't look back. I was horrified. I mean, I knew he was unpredictable but…"

"Unpredictable? Honey, that isn't 'unpredictable' where I come from. 'Unpredictable' means when is my son going to lose his best jacket or will the Yankees win the pennant." Percy chewed more food, deep in thought. "I remember reading about some punk killing an old guy in a liquor store over thirty-six bucks. So that was Danny?"

Lily nodded then picked up one of the corners of the apron she'd been wearing to wipe teary, red eyes.

Percy took a large forkful of string beans and shoved them in her mouth. "These are good. What did you season them with? Besides bacon grease?"

Lily sat up straighter and began to talk, almost in rote. "Two tablespoons strained bacon fat and clarified butter, with a clove of minced garlic. After the beans are blanched in a little water --"

"What's that?" Percy interrupted.

"Blanching? You drop vegetables in boiling water for a minute or two to help keep their color. Then you remove them. After that, you sauté the beans in the mixture for a few more minutes, throw on salt, pepper, crumbled bacon bits and bake the beans, covered, in a low heat oven for twenty minutes."

"You sound like you could teach a class in this cooking stuff."

Lily smiled but didn't look up. "I guess."

"So, what happened after you drove off?"

"I was told a squad car was rounding the corner right as I was leaving. The police didn't see me but they saw Danny shouting on the sidewalk and waving the gun. They arrested him before he could get away."

"This Danny's lucky they didn't shoot him. Cops have been known to do that with less provocation. So you got off scot free?"

"I wouldn't say that. I still have nightmares over it." Lily let out a deep sigh and looked away, hands shaking in her lap.

"The upshot is," Percy said, mopping up gravy with a piece of roll she snagged from a plate at the center of the table. "Danny Deluca is in jail awaiting trial for murder and the cops don't know about you."

"They know. But they didn't believe it when Danny said I was with him."

"And why was that?"

"I denied it and my father said I was home all night. Dad even paid one of the servants to swear to it. I think Hanson suspected, but he didn't say anything."

"Hanson?"

"The butler. He's been with us since I can remember. Our lawyer maintained Danny was lying because I'd broken up with him."

Percy let out a chuckle. "You wrapped that one up and tied it with a neat little bow."

"Danny said if he ever got out, he would pay me back for leaving him on the sidewalk. He said if I'd been there he wouldn't have gotten caught." She let out a strangled sob. "My life is such a mess."

"That it is, sister, and you're not even out of your teens." Percy picked up a whole roll, slathered it with butter, took a bite, and rolled her eyes. "God, I love butter. You make these rolls?"

Lily nodded, wiping at her nose. Percy chewed thoughtfully.

"I didn't know a meal so good could come from this kitchen, but don't mention that to Mother. I'm going to pass on the apple pie. I'd like to be able to roll over in the morning." She brushed crumbs off her shirt and hands. "Okay, Lily. First, we need to find out if Danny's still in jail. Although even if he's free, why would he shoot Connie? Why not shoot you? You're the one he's got it in for."

"Danny was always the jealous type. He said if he caught me with another man, he'd kill the both of us. If he was out, maybe he saw us in the window last night."

"Honey, all of New York might of seen you in the window. But you're thinking this might be Danny's inventive way of getting back at you? From what you've been telling me, he doesn't sound like a man with those kind of brains, but I'll check it out." She turned and leaned in to the girl sitting beside her.

"Being I'm practically old enough to be your mother...ah...mother's younger best friend, I'm going to give you a piece of unsolicited advice. You want to reach thirty?

Tame it down a little." Percy stood up and carried her plate to the kitchen sink. "Thanks for the grub, kiddo. Soon I'll be tipping the scale at two-hundred pounds if you stick around here much longer." She said over her shoulder to Lily, "You want to bring me those dirty dishes?"

"Sure." Lily rose and began to clear the table. Her voice had a forced quality. "Speaking of sticking around, how long do you think I'll have to stay here?"

"Getting tired of us already?"

Lily's face registered surprise and embarrassment. "I didn't mean…"

"Never mind, kid. That's just my sense of humor."

Lily gave Percy a little smile, more in acceptance than understanding. "You're an odd woman, if you don't mind my saying."

Percy let out a guffaw. She picked up a dishcloth and soap and reached into the soapy water in the sink. "I don't mind. Take as good as you give, that's my motto. I'll wash, you dry."

Lily nodded.

Percy went on, "In answer to your question, I'm not sure when we'll wrap this up. Hopefully, in a few days, but this is the best place for you until then. But no more trying to buy us Christmas trees or anything like that, although the food is appreciated. Your father is paying for you to be stashed away. This just happens to be the place." She stopped washing and turned to the girl. "And while you're here--"

"I know. I'm to stay in Oliver's room, not use the phone, don't write any letters, and don't answer the door."

"Right." Percy went back to washing dishes. "But you don't have to stay in your room, unless you want to. The folks seem to like you and if you're feeling sociable…" Percy stopped talking and shrugged her shoulders. "Your call."

They worked in silence for a few minutes. Lily turned to Percy in a tentative manner.

"You don't happen to know when or if I'll get my evening bag back, do you? I'd just bought it a few hours before all this happened and it cost me four-hundred dollars. Not that the money --"

"Four hundred bucks," Percy interrupted. "For a ratty little purse?"

Lily threw back her head and laughed. "It's not 'ratty'. The mesh is made of sterling silver and the clasp is covered with a piece of sixteenth century jade, museum quality. It was a Christmas present to myself. I found it at a Chinese art auction."

"The last purse I bought cost me a buck fifty-two. Black plastic with a Lucite clasp, found at the Five and Dime."

The smile faded from Lily's face as recognition took its place. "Oh. I'm sorry. I didn't mean to sound like…" Her voice faded out, shame taking its place.

"A privileged character?" Percy's voice was even and non-judgmental. "Don't worry about it. We are what we are. No point in feeling bad about something we can't help."

Without looking up from the dishtowel, Lily said in a quiet voice, "I hate my life."

"So you say."

"Yes, I say." The girl's voice was small and childlike.

"Then do something about it."

Lily sighed and wiped away a tear. "It's easier said than done."

"Anything worthwhile is. I found that little ditty in a fortune cookie once. That's been *my* foray into Chinese art."

Lily's head snapped around and she stared at Percy openmouthed, astonishment written all over her face. Then she burst out laughing.

Percy threw the dishrag on the back of the sink and dried her hands. "Finish up in here, will you? I'm going to visit with my son before he goes to sleep."

She crossed to the swinging door but stopped at the sound of Lily's voice, now powerful and certain.

"You're lucky, you know that?" Percy turned around. Lily faced her from across the large kitchen, looking much older than her eighteen years. "You have a family that loves you. There aren't any diamonds in the world that can match that."

Percy stared at her, appraisingly. Lily stared back, unwavering.

"You kill that elf, Lily?" Percy asked in a soft voice.

Lily pulled air into her lungs with a sound of shock and frustration. "I told you already. I'll take an oath on a Bible if you want; I swear on my dead mother's grave. No, I didn't kill him. And his name is…was…Connie." She glared at Percy much the way Sera did when she was exasperated with her older sister, just stopping short of sticking her tongue out in anger.

Percy grinned. "Just checking. You can't be too sure with an eight-year old in the house."

* * * *

Being in the closest room to the front door and a light sleeper, Percy heard the knocking before anyone else. She slipped out of bed, threw on her robe, and gave a quick glance to make sure Oliver hadn't been awakened. Shivering a little, she fiddled with the locks and threw open the front door just as the knocking turned into pounding. Detective Kenneth Hutchers stood before her, knuckle-fisted, a grim look on his face.

"I was beginning to think nobody was home. Doesn't your doorbell work?" He brushed past Percy and wheeled around, staring at her as if she was the intruder.

"Not since 1935 and keep it down, Hutchers. What time is it?"

He looked at his watch. "Four-thirty. I've been up since two."

"Well, good for you. The rest of us are still sleeping. What do you want?"

"This is going to wake you up good. The Christmas angel's dead, murdered. They found her body somewhere around midnight. We don't think it was robbery."

"Keep your voice down, I said. And take off your hat. I don't like people wearing hats inside my house." Distracted, he took of his plaid, wood cap, while Percy gave a quick glance down the hall to the room where Lily was.

If Lily comes out to see what all the commotion is, I'm dead.

"Let's go into the parlor." She turned to the room across from her bedroom, switched on the overhead light, and motioned for him to follow.

The largest room in the apartment, the fifteen by twenty-five foot room was spattered here and there with more of her great-aunt's ornate furniture. A comfortable-looking but faded brocade sofa with matching chair and ottoman dominated the section of the room nearest the door. A radio console sat next to one end of the sofa. On the opposite wall, two smaller, wood carved chairs faced an octagon inlay tea table, still set with checkerboard and checkers. Badly done paintings of pastoral scenes and imaginary French aristocrats stared back at them, remnants of Mother's temporary plunge into the world of art. Another one of her hobbies gone awry, they filled wall space bringing forth little appreciation, but much amusement.

Emerald-colored ferns hung luxuriantly in each of the large windows, living odes to Mother's more accomplished diversion, her green thumb. At one of the far corners, two still-life peacocks strutted on the golden background of an opulent room divider. Behind the screen sat her father's dark oak desk and file cabinets, well oiled but worn.

In the past, most of the room had functioned as office for Cole Investigations. That was before Gilleathain's death and age and illness had its way with Pop. Cole Investigations was pushed farther and farther into the corner of the parlor by the realities of life and the needs of a growing family. Maybe with Percy assuming the partnership loss, the business might resurrect itself. Maybe.

Percy crossed over to a mock Tiffany floor lamp wearing a large, half-domed, multi-colored stained glass shade. She pulled on the chain and the room was illuminated in a burst of soft, warm colors replacing the strident white of the overhead fixture.

Percy closed the door and turned to Hutchers. "So talk to me. What dead Christmas angel?"

"The broad from Santa Land. She was dressed up like a Christmas angel and like I said, we don't think it was a robbery gone bad. She was still wearing her earrings, diamonds and pearls. Coroner said they looked real. And she had ten bucks tucked in her bosom." He took out a notepad and read from it. "Gertrude Kunkle, forty-nine years old, accountant for Harry Wienblatt. Still in her costume, just like the elf. Skull crushed by a heavy object, maybe a brick; something like that. We'll know more after the doc gives her a once over. I guess Santa's next. What a Christmas."

"Where'd this happen? Santa Land?"

Hutchers nodded and Percy went over to the small fireplace and wiped the dust off the alabaster mantle with the edge of her sleeve. A nervous habit, she always tidied things when she was stressed or trying to think fast.

"Cleaning lady found her body at midnight." Hutchers went on, "Gertie was crammed inside the gingerbread house."

"What made the cleaning woman look in there?"

"She said the statue of Mrs. Clause was lying on the floor. When she went to upright it, she found the body. The cleaning lady must have polished off half a bottle of Irish whisky before we got there. What the hell is going on?"

"How the hell should I know?"

Hutchers' glance was accusatory, as if Percy had some inside knowledge. She did, but glared back at him on general principles. It was a stalemate.

The detective was the first to break the silence. "I know it's that crazy kid, Lily Waller. She's still on the loose and she's killed again." His look was one of defiance, like 'tell me I'm wrong.'

Percy kept as much emotion from her face as she could, knowing the girl was asleep down the hall in her son's room.

If nothing else, this clears Lily of the elf's murder.

She was surprised at her relief. Maybe she'd had more doubts about Lily than she admitted.

"What makes you think the 'crazy kid' did it? You find another one of her handbags under the body, this time with a brick in it?"

"Very funny. But who else could it be?"

She didn't answer, but changed the subject. "Who's Danny DeLuca? You know anything about him?"

His eyes narrowed. "The kid who escaped from Rikers yesterday? Why do you ask? Is he with the girl? I know they had something going at one time. If you know something, you'd better start talking. You could be an accessory."

Percy plopped down in a chair and threw her slippered feet up on the coffee table. Nonchalance was her middle name. "I just read about this DeLuca in the newspapers, that's all, and thought you might know something about it. Sit down; take a load off."

Hutchers remained by the door. "No thanks. I'm on my way home. I pick up the kids in a couple of hours. I only came over to tell you about this, in case you know more than you're

spilling. She's killed two people now." He looked down at the cap in his hand. "I'm sorry I involved you. Winds up, I didn't do you or Jude a favor. You'd better watch yourself."

"I'll keep that in mind." Percy stood, strode to the parlor door, and opened it in a dismissive manner. "If that's all, I'd like to get back to sleep. Thanks for dropping by with the cheery news."

He didn't move but stood looking Percy up and down. Embarrassed, Percy drew the orange, black, and white print kimono robe Mother made tight around her, holding it closed at the neck and waist.

"What?"

"I don't know, Perce. You look different."

"Of course, I look different, Hutchers. You woke me up in the middle of the night. Give me a break, will you?"

"No, no, I didn't mean…. It's just with your hair down loose and that silky robe on, you look feminine. You know, like a woman."

Jesus Christ, what an idiot.

"I've got a news flash for you. I am a woman. I've got the son to prove it. Now get out."

He moved closer and stood in front of her, staring into her eyes. She stared back unflinching. "You're a fine-looking woman, Perce, if you don't mind my saying."

"You're the second person to ask me if I mind what they're saying. I'm starting to find it annoying." She backed up and gestured to the front door with her thumb in a fisted hand. "Merry Christmas and so long, Hutchers. Don't let the door hit your backside on the way out."

"Always the tough broad, right?"

"Always the tough cop, right?"

He smiled at her. "This isn't over. You're hiding something. I can tell."

She smiled back. "Right now I'm hiding a yawn."

He laughed. "Okay, *Miss* Cole, you win. I'll go, but if it looks like you know anything, I'll be back."

"Call first. Alexander Graham Bell can use the dough."

The detective walked out into the hall, and left without a backward glance, the front door closing with a dull sound. Percy was drawn to it and studied the locks. Something dawned on her. She didn't have to unlock the same number of locks to let Hutchers in as she'd locked before going to bed.

Percy's head whipped around to the coat rack. Both Lily's hat and coat were missing. She ran down the hall to Oliver's room, threw the door open and flipped on the overhead light. The room was as empty as the mussed bed.

Don't panic, kid. Check the whole house first.

In case Lily and Sera had decided to have a pajama party in the middle of the night – as girls sometimes do -- Percy went to Sera's room and opened the door a crack. There her sister was sleeping in her usual position, lying on her back, atop the bed covers, clutching her pillow in both arms. No Lily. Percy checked the kitchen then the bathroom. Still no Lily.

Okay, time to panic. You're a first-class chump, Persephone Cole. She's gone and you're left holding the bag.

Chapter Fourteen

"What's going on, Persephone?"

Percy, having shut the bathroom door harder than she'd intended, spun around to see her father in his chair, wheeling himself out of her parent's bedroom. Dressed in pajamas, he had his robe loosely belted, his bad leg covered with a small rug.

"Didn't mean to wake you, Pop."

"I don't sleep as good as I used to. Don't worry about it. But what's going on?"

"Let's go into the parlor, Pop. Something's happened." She half pushed, half followed his chair as it silently rolled down the hallway. She could feel her heart pounding in her chest, but tried to control it.

She started to close the parlor door but was stopped by her father. "Leave the door open, Persephone. I'm a light sleeper these days, but I want to hear if this woke anyone else up. We'll keep our voices down." He folded his hands in his lap. "Now who was here?"

"Detective Kenneth Hutchers just left. There's been another murder, Pop. This time a woman who was filling in at Santa Land as the Christmas angel. Coshed on the head. I don't have many details but he came to tell me. He thinks I know more than I'm telling, which I do."

"This tied in with the elf killing?"

She nodded but looked away. "There's more." She looked at her father. "Lily's gone and I don't know where or for how long. All I know is she's not in the apartment." Percy began to pace. "I'm a dope, Pop, a real dope. I should have never believed her or been taken in by the money. For all I know, she killed both these people and I'm stashing a murderer in our home. And with my son --"

"Persephone, don't get yourself in an upset," Pop interrupted. "We don't know anything yet."

He opened his mouth to continue, when they both heard the rattle of one of the locks on the front door. Percy and Pop turned and saw the front door open just enough for Lily's head to peek in, snow covered hat dripping wet flakes on the floor. Not seeing father or daughter, a hunched over Lily crept inside careful and slow, making as little noise as possible.

Wordless, Percy crossed over to a closet in the parlor, took out her son's baseball bat, and held it in a menacing manner. "You!" she said in a hushed but threatening voice to Lily. "Get in here."

Startled and scared, Lily jerked her body upright and emitted a slight cry, slushy snow spilling onto her shoulders and the floor.

"I...I..." she said, eyes focused on the bat in Percy's hands.

"You've got ten-seconds to tell me where you've been, and then I'm making no promises for what I do to you." Fury covered Percy's face. She reached out, grabbed Lily by one of the shoulder pads of her coat, and dragged her into the room, leaving the door slightly ajar.

Lily stumbled inside, saying, "I...I...I'm sorry. I went out for a walk. I know you told me not to --"

"You're damn straight I told you not to. So you went out for a walk, did you? Maybe, maybe not. Maybe you took a cab to Fifty-ninth and Fifth. Maybe you killed the Christmas angel. Did you? Not that I am going to believe anything you say anymore." She stepped forward. Lily backed away.

"No, no. I just went for a walk. In the snow. It's snowing. I wanted to be in the snow."

Pop put his arm out in front of Percy. "Hold on, Persephone. Let her talk. And you'd better make it good, child, or I will personally dial the police department and have them come to pick you up."

"Please don't do that, Mr. Cole. I didn't do anything. What Christmas angel? What are you talking about? I just went out for a walk. I --"

"How'd you get back in?" Percy demanded to know. "Where'd you get that key?" She pointed with the narrow end of the bat at the key still clutched in Lily's hand.

"Sera gave it to me. I swear! I told her about my claustrophobia. I got locked in a closet once when I was a kid. I can't be cooped up inside for long, not even in here. So when I told Sera, she gave me this extra key. I can't go to jail. Please don't send me. I'd go crazy."

Percy and Pop stared at her, their faces riddled with doubt.

Lily went on, her voice desperate and beseeching. "I just went out for a walk! I wasn't gone more than a half an hour, I swear. I don't know anything about an angel. I swear." She started to cry.

"Stop that bawling, Lily, or I'll slug you for sure," Percy said. "I'm sick of your pathetic act. Now take off your coat and hand it over to Pop, easy like. You make one quick move and I hit a home run using your head. You got me?"

Face drained of color, Lily nodded once and unbuttoned her coat. She walked over slowly keeping her eye on Percy and the bat. She handed the coat to Pop. He looked at Percy for further instructions.

"Pop, search the pockets. Give him your hat, too, just in case you've got something hidden in there, sister."

"I don't, I swear." She handed the hat over, nonetheless.

"You also swore you'd stay inside," Percy countered.

"There's nobody outside now to see me, honest. The streets are deserted. How could it have hurt?" Lily wasn't making any noise, but a stream of tears flowed down her strained face.

"Detective Hutchers was here, kid. You know, the cop who issued a warrant for your arrest? That's who's out on the streets. It seems a woman was killed tonight, wearing one of the Santa Land costumes. Only this time, her head got smashed in - maybe by you - not far away from where Connie's murder was committed."

"Golly!" Lily, jaw slack and wide-eyed, crumpled into one of the chairs.

"There's nothing in here but a hanky, Persephone," said Pop in a quiet voice. "Nothing else."

"And the key. That's all I had with me. I wanted some fresh air. It started to snow. I love the snow," she added wistfully.

"Go pack your things and get out." Percy's face was grim and her voice devoid of emotion.

"But where will I go?"

"I don't care where you go. You've got the money; check into the Ritz."

"Shouldn't we take a vote on it?" The voice came from the other side of the doorframe. Sera stood there in a hot pink bathrobe and fluffy slippers. "After all, I'm the one that gave her the key."

Three pair of eyes turned to Serendipity, who marched into the room.

"Percy, this isn't fair. You're not being fair." Percy opened her mouth to speak, but Sera went on in a rush. "I told Lily to do it if she felt closed in. You can't throw her out because of what I did."

"Persephone, really my dear, a person has a right to walk in new fallen snow. It's so peaceful and Christmassy."

Mother walked into the room, her checkered robe open, worn, leather slippers slapping on the wood floor.

"Now, Mother," was all Percy managed to get out before everyone started talking at the same time.

The level of voices rose, as each person tried to be heard about the rest until a yelp overrode everyone.

"Hey!" All turned to see Oliver, sleepy-eyed, barefoot and clad only in pajamas, standing in the doorway. "What's going on? You woke me up."

Percy was the first to recover. "Oliver, sweetie! Come here to mommy." She set down the bat, picked him up and cuddled him in her arms, letting out a sound of the effort. "Whoa! You're getting to be such a big boy. I can hardly lift you." She turned away from the others. "Let's get you back to bed."

"No!" The boy struggled to get down. "I don't want Lily to go anywhere either, Mommy. I like her."

"I know, Oliver, but --"

Everyone started to talk again. Pop picked up the baseball bat and banged on the floor for attention. "Enough. I want everyone to be quiet and listen to me." He looked at his eldest daughter, who opened her mouth to talk. "You, too, Persephone." He turned to Lily. "What you did, young lady, was foolish. And you disobeyed very explicit instructions." Lily also started to reply but Pop held up his hand. "Nobody speaks right now but me. Understood?"

Lily nodded, and looked down, shame written all over her face.

"Serendipity, you need to learn some manners and respect. And don't *you* open your mouth and sass me. You're not too big for me to turn you over my knee. Your sister is supporting this family right now. She is keeping a roof over our heads. You are to respect what she says, in particular, anything regarding her cases. You do not undermine them. Understood?"

Serendipity shuffled from one hot pink slipper to the other but nodded and looked down.

"Mother, you are a wonderful woman and anytime you want to take over your kitchen again, you go right ahead and do so. It was very generous of you to let Lily usurp your place while she's here, not that anyone could, my dear, ever take your place," he added in a warm, loving tone.

"Oh, Father, what a sweet thing to say." Mother beamed at her husband. "I find I am enjoying not being responsible for the kitchen right now. It gives me a chance to catch up on my Christmas knitting. I've been working on your present, Father, although I can't remember if it's knit one, purl two or knit two, purl one. It's so confusing. And you know, Father, Lily is a very good cook."

Father nodded at her words and turned to Percy. "Persephone, you are completely right in everything you said." Percy looked at him in astonishment. "But this being Christmas and all, with good will toward men and young women, I might add, I am going to ask you to give Lily one more chance under the proviso that she obey you to the letter on everything you say from now on. We will start anew. What do you say, daughter?"

Everyone turned and stared at Percy, who stood tall and angry. Finally, Percy nodded and let out a deep breath. "Okay."

"Yah!" Oliver let out a cheer and everyone in the room visibly relaxed. "Can we have some bacon and scrambled eggs right now? I'm hungry." Oliver looked from one person to the other, ending with his mother.

"It's a little early, but if you're hungry...." Percy stopped talking and grinned at her son.

"I could make breakfast, if you'd like Miss Cole." Lily stepped forward, looking eager to please.

"Can you do French toast?" Mother walked over to Lilly, reached out and locked arms with the girl. A grateful look crossed Lily's face and she nodded. Arm in arm, they left for the kitchen, trailed by Sera. Mother's ethereal voice drifted back into the parlor, as she nattered on.

"I haven't had French toast in over a year. I can't quite get the hang of it. I mean, do you toast the bread first and then dip it in beaten eggs? But when I do that it's such a mess. Whatever I do, though, it never comes out quite right. I've got some maple syrup all the way from Vermont in the back of the larder I've been saving. We can put that on top. I think French toast – made correctly -- with maple syrup is a bit of heaven on earth, don't you?"

Before Oliver left, he turned to his mother. "I know Lily disobeyed you, Mommy, but I do too sometimes, and you forgive me. Everybody makes mistakes now and then," he added in a very grownup manner.

Percy and Pop watched the boy leave and there was a moment of silence. Percy shut the door and looked at her father.

"That's a wonderful little boy, Persephone. He does you credit."

"He does us all credit, but I hope we did the right thing, Pop. This whole thing scares me, harboring a felon."

"Persephone, put your fears about Oliver and the rest of us aside for a moment, so you can think clearly. What does your gut tell you about this girl? Does she strike you as the type of person who would kill two people in cold blood?"

"Pop, given the right set of circumstances, anybody could turn into a killer."

"No, no, no. We're talking about this girl, this set of circumstances. Think about it."

Percy closed her eyes and thought for a moment. When she opened them, she looked at her father with a smile. "In answer to your question, I don't think she'd commit murders

quite so crude. I think she'd plan it out. And these have all the earmarks of being on the fly. Spontaneous."

"Crimes of passion?"

"Yeah. And something inside me says if that was the case, Lily would honest enough to 'fess up to it. So no, I don't think it's her. But she's a loose cannon, Pop. If she does something else stupid and the cops find out we're hiding her, she could get us into a lot of trouble. At the very least, we could both lose our licenses." She came closer and knelt before her father. Close up, she saw his fevered eyes and waxy skin tone. "You don't look so good, Pop. I think your Custer's Last Stand took a lot out of you."

"Maybe so."

"What happened when you called the doctor about the series of penicillin shots? What did he say?"

"I go into the hospital day after tomorrow. With all the wounded soldiers, there isn't a bed until then. Meanwhile, I'm supposed to keep taking my pain-killers." He let out a laugh. "I'm loaded up with them. I don't think I could stand, even if I wanted to."

"December twenty-first? Did he say how long he thought you'd be there?" *Jesus, what a lousy Christmas. Pop in the hospital fighting for his leg, maybe his life.*

"Doc told me we'd pretty much know right away if the penicillin was going to work or not. At least this way, my leg has a fighting chance." He looked at his daughter. "It's all thanks to you, Percy, and that money you gave me."

Guilt rode over Percy like a steamroller. "Pop, there's something I've got to tell you. Mr. Waller promised me more money if I could keep Lily out of jail. Five thousand dollars. That's why she's here."

Pop didn't answer but gave out with a soft whistle.

"I wanted the money for a fresh start for Oliver and me. Our own home, a little savings, a future for Oliver. I wasn't thinking straight, Pop."

"Five thousand dollars could do that."

"I shouldn't have agreed to the deal without talking to you first. Twenty-five hundred should go to you, an equal split. I was being selfish."

"I don't want your money, Persephone."

"Regardless, Pop. It isn't right. We're partners. Or I want us to be. But I got carried away, got greedy. I'm sorry."

Pop smiled at his daughter. "As Oliver says, everybody makes mistakes now and then."

Percy let out a laugh. "He is quite a boy, isn't he?"

"That he is. And if you move out, I'll miss him. But it's probably the right thing to do, Persephone. You're still a young woman --"

"Not so young, Pop," Percy interrupted. "I'll be thirty-six in April."

"That's young from where I'm sitting. Besides, my girl, you've always been a late bloomer. Why, you didn't marry until you were twenty-seven. Then you had Oliver. Mother had two babies before she was twenty-one."

"But she didn't have Sera until fifteen years later."

"Exactly. You never know what life is going to hand you."

"Or throw at you." Percy and her father laughed. "Thanks, Pop, for understanding. Maybe part of my harshness with Lily has been a guilty conscience over the five thousand smackers."

"That much money can throw anyone."

"There's a drawback to everything."

"Truer words were never spoke. To change the subject, I got some answers on the census report you wanted on the building at Fifty-ninth Street. My friend dropped it off on his way home. When you kick people out of rent-controlled apartments, you have to file a lot of papers, dot your 'i's and cross your 't's. And I got a copy of the police report, too."

"How'd you wangle that?"

"It pays to stay friends with your partners from the good old days." Pop wheeled his chair to the Peacock screen, disappearing behind it.

Chapter Fifteen

He looked up at the four-story building, slick and wet, from across the potholed pavement. Dim streetlights provided a scant amount of illumination in the night sky and the falling snow, just starting to stick, obscured even more. He'd followed the nosy, large woman in the man's hat hours ago, all the way up to seventy-second street and then down to the lower east side.

He'd been outside her apartment house all night, watching everyone come and go. He'd seen the scruffy police detective, the one who was investigating the murders, enter a short time ago. He'd been surprised by that. Do not underestimate the large woman, he said to himself.

He'd watched Lily leave slightly before the policeman came. He'd thought about her; that Jezebel, that whore, that daughter of Satan. She'd reentered shortly after the cop left. Tempted though he'd been to silence her when he could, he'd never left his position. It was not time.

He stood, impervious to the cold, rain, snow, and lack of sleep. They meant nothing to him. He mused for a moment, as the silent snow fell on his head and his numb ears, before pulling back into the shelter of the doorway.

An abandoned building across the street from his quarry was ideal. He was protected. He was nurtured. It was only right.

What was the large woman up to? Why did the detective come to see her at such an hour? Was he having an affair with her, the woman who couldn't seem to mind her own business? Unless stopped, she might cause all kinds of trouble.

And what was the girl doing here, as well? She, too, should be stopped. Especially her.

He looked at his watch, straining his eyes in the dark. He was tired and felt older than he could imagine, but he would sleep later when the job was done. He would sleep later.

Chapter Sixteen

"What is it, Persephone? What are you looking at?"

Pop put down the papers on his desk and rolled his chair over to the window facing the street. His hand reached up and absentmindedly stroked a delicate frond of a cascading fern. "Do you see something?"

She shook her head and shivered. "No, Pop, I don't think so. But I can't shake the feeling…" She stopped speaking, drew back the white sheer drape again, and peered out into the darkness speckled with the white of falling snow.

What she really wanted was a cigarette, but that was something you didn't tell Pop. He thought it was a nasty habit, not glamorous, not sexy, but smelly. She rarely smoked. It was expensive and not worth the price, as a rule. But tonight, with so much going on, she could use the calming influence. She thought about the pack in the glove compartment of the car. Stale, probably, but half full. It beckoned to her like a slice of pecan pie. She licked her lips in anticipation.

"I thought I saw something earlier but nothing's there now. Never mind, Pop. I've got the willies from this business, that's all. Let's go over the list again, see if I missed anything."

Percy pulled herself from the window and sat down in the chair beside her father's desk. He followed, rolling back to the desk and settling in. Pop picked up the reports again.

"There's not much here, really," he said. "Between the Census Bureau and the logs of the Department of Rent control, everyone is accounted for, gone or soon going."

"Your friend makes good copies, so detailed, almost as good as reading the original."

"Renaldi studied calligraphy, you know. He prides himself on being able to copy anyone's handwriting exactly. Most times you can't tell the difference."

"It's a good thing he didn't turn to a life of crime, Pop."

"With his mother? She'd skin him alive." He laughed at the memory of his friend's overbearing mother then cleared his throat. "To sum it up, the last of the long-term lease tenants moved out six-months ago, each family receiving five-hundred dollars in compensation."

Percy's eyebrows shot up in surprise.

"I know," her father agreed. "Most people don't see that kind of money all in one fell swoop in their lifetimes."

"So they didn't balk about leaving."

"Good grief, no. This was a godsend for most of them. It's not the same for the small businesses on the ground floor, five exactly, including the cobbler and watch repair you spoke to. There's no compensation for them, and they have more to lose. Their leases end December thirty-first. Demolition starts the day after New Year's."

"What about this line right here? What did he write here?" She pointed to an almost unreadable line on the mirror copy of the nineteen-forty census document. "Could that word be janitor?"

"What are you talking about? Where?" Pop grabbed his bifocals, twisted the neck of his desk lamp for better light, leaned in, and scrutinized the paper.

"I think this is somebody's name," Percy insisted. "Maybe Ernie, and over to the right might be the word janitor."

"Is that what you think it reads?" He looked doubtful. "This line doesn't even look like writing. It looks like someone scribbling around seeing if the pen worked. Or maybe it's a mistake and scratched out."

"I don't know, Pop. It's been a while since you've read a child's handwriting. I try to decipher Oliver's penmanship all the time. Sometimes it looks just like this."

"You think a child wrote on an official government document?"

"A child or an uneducated man."

"Phew." Pop blew out air dramatically. "You're clutching at straws, Persephone, and I have no idea why. What makes you think the building and its demise has anything to do with these two murders, anyway?" He rolled his wheelchair back and wiped sweat from his brow. "I'm sorry, Persephone. I'm being no help to you. I have to lie down. I'm tired."

Percy jumped up. "Of course, you do, Pop, and I'm sorry for haranguing you about this. You're probably right. It's just scrawl. You rest and we'll try not to disturb you."

She hurried his chair to the parlor door, opened it wide, and watched him push himself slowly to his bedroom. Then Percy grabbed her keys, threw on her coat over her robe, and went out, quietly closing the door behind her.

Chapter Seventeen

Percy buttoned her coat against the falling snow and hopped down from the stoop onto the sidewalk. She could feel the icy slush through her slippers and chided herself for not changing into her boots.

Aw, nuts. They're going to be soaked through. Oh, well. The car is only across the street. I'll dry them on the radiator when I get back. Nobody will ever know. Exactly what Lily thought, I'll bet. For the first time in years, Percy felt like a wayward teenager sneaking a smoke.

One or two people were up, heading off to somewhere, but not as many as usual, it being a lousy day. When your life is working and paying your bills, you use any reason to stay in bed an extra minute or two, and the snowfall had offered just that. Soon kids would be out, playing in the slush before going to school wet and cold, warmed by their youth and enthusiasm. But for now, the street was Percy's.

A car motor started up, as she crossed the sidewalk and stepped down into the curb. Looking both ways into the dark, deserted street, she vaguely wondered where the running motor sound was coming from. She dismissed it; the call of the cigarettes too strong.

She turned sideways, jammed herself between two snow-covered parked cars, and stepped out into the street. Bright headlights to her left came on and a car pulled out from the row. It idled for a moment then she heard the revving of the motor, followed by the squeal of tires.

Now, who would be burning rubber at this hour?

Her body swiveled in the direction of the sound. Blinded by the on-coming blaze of light, she froze like a deer caught in its headlights. Only her hand seemed able to move, flying up to shield her eyes from the sudden glare. When she tried to flee back to the curb, soggy slippers weighed her feet down, adhered to the snowy asphalt almost like glue.

At the last second, she threw herself, shoeless, onto the slippery hood of the nearest parked car, the hardness of the surface taking her breath away. Only her feet jutted out in the street. She felt the whip of the passing car's radio antenna on her toes as it careened by. The slap caused her body to rotate like a top and her cheek hit the windshield with a smack. A screech of metal against metal assaulted her eardrums, as the car parked in front was sideswiped by the renegade vehicle. With closed eyes, she heard it speed away until there was only the sound of her beating heart.

Time seemed to slow down as Percy listened to this, clinging to the windshield wiper to keep from sliding to the ground. After a moment of silence, she released her grip, rolled onto her belly, and slid to the frosty pavement, feet first. The cold felt good on her hot, stinging toes, hopefully bruised but not broken. They were painful to say the least. She stood for a moment; her feet submerged in the quiet slush until numbness set in. Then Percy leaned against the car, and tried to figure out what the hell that was all about. Bad driver? Or bad murder attempt?

Number two gets my vote.

* * * *

Sera was coming from the kitchen just as Percy reentered the apartment. On seeing her kid sister, Percy paused, panting, unsure of what to say. Her disheveled and drenched appearance made Sera suck in a breath so long and noisy that in the middle of it, Percy held a finger to her lips.

"Shush," Percy added in a low voice.

Sera clapped a hand over her mouth and ran down the hallway toward her sister. Both stood and watched the closed kitchen door, waiting a beat. Satisfied no one heard, they turned to one another.

"What happened to you?" Sera's voice was not quite a stage whisper, closer to a growl.

"You look terrible."

"Let's just say, I went out for a smoke."

Sera looked down at her older sister's red, swollen feet. "Barefoot?"

"About that, Sera. Are you giving me slippers again this Christmas? I sure hope so."

"What's going on, Percy?" Sera searched Percy's face. "Is that a bruise coming up on your cheek? Are you okay? You look terrible."

"You already said that. Don't say it again." She paused and thought. "How bad do I look, really?"

"Like you got hit by a truck."

"Close enough."

Percy began to hobble down the hallway. "Ah, Sera, mind giving me a hand to the bathroom? My toes are a little stiff. I think I'll take a long, hot soak, loosen them up a bit."

"Sure," Sera said, wrapping a protective arm around Percy's waist. "You just lean on me, Percy." Sera moved both of them toward the bathroom, trying to get in step with Percy.

"All right, I will." She put her arm around Sera's shoulder and distributed some of her weight onto the smaller woman.

"But not too much. I'm not as strong as I look."

Percy glanced down at her sister and visibly restrained a hoot of laughter. Sera began to giggle.

"Sorry about this," Percy said, taking a few steps. "My feet are not what they should be."

"Never you mind, Sis. I've got you. You lean on me all you want. That's what sisters are for," Sera said with a burst of pride.

"Thank you, Sera." Percy's tone was serious and grateful.

Never thought the day would come when I'd be leaning on Sera. Never say never, like Mother says.

They came to the bathroom door. Percy pushed it open with a free hand and flipped on the wall light switch. It was a large twelve by twelve room, white subway tiles running up the walls finished off in a black and white trim. The floor was covered with smaller black and white tiles done in a herringbone pattern, laid by immigrant workers short on cash and long on talent, made to last forever.

Mother added a touch of color with a handmade yellow rag rug, and yellow towels. The toilet was in a corner, the white enamel tank topped with one of Mother's more recent projects, a southern belle doll wearing a crocheted yellow hoop skirt, discretely covering a roll of toilet paper. Over the white pedestal sink, was a mirrored medicine cabinet and above that, a pull-chain light, which had never worked since day one. Against a longer wall, a huge claw-foot bathtub, in need of resurfacing, sat beneath a makeshift round shower curtain, hanging from the ceiling on two chains. Slung over the white cloth shower curtain and bunched up to one side was a pair of Sera's stockings. Two of Oliver's toys, a rubber duck and a sailboat, waited on the rim of the tub for the return of the small boy. Percy loved this bathroom and often studied the craftsmanship of it as she laid back in her bubble bath. She would make an effort to concentrate on that instead of her toes.

"I think a long soak in a hot tub will do me good. I'll be fine in an hour or so. Thanks so much. I'll take it from here." She sucked in a breath between clench teeth as she moved away, her painful feet getting to her.

"No siree Bob. You sit on the john, Percy, I'll run the water." Not letting go, Sera walked her sister over to the commode, and plopped her down on the closed lid. She crossed to the tub, crammed the plug in the drain, and turned on the hot water tap, chatting all the time.

"I've even got some new bath salts – lavender -- I'll share with you. And you don't have to worry about getting out until you want to, either. I don't need to take a bath every single morning. I remember reading somewhere in the Ozarks they don't bathe but once a week. Of course, Oliver will want to come in before he goes to school, but that's not for an hour or so. And I promise not to say anything about this to the folks." She poured the powder into the running water, floral scent filling the air. "Smell that? Yummy!"

"Thank you for taking care of me, Sera." Percy's voice was soft and vulnerable.

Sera brushed her off. "Oh, you don't have to thank --"

"Yes, I do," Percy said, cutting her off. "It's appreciated."

Pleased but embarrassed, Sera looked away. "It's the least I can do, Percy." She went back to her sister and handed her a hair clip she took from the pocket of her robe.

"Put your hair up with this clip and stand. Let's get you out of these wet things." A bedraggled Percy obeyed on both counts while Sera went on, "After all, I'm the one who encouraged Lily to go outside, and I'm sure whatever happened to you out there was my fault in some way. It always is."

Percy sloughed off the wet robe and pajamas as Sera picked up dropping clothes. A nude Percy turned and smiled at her sister.

"Nope, not this time. I think I brought this one on myself." She walked on her heels over to the tub, stroked the warm water with one hand and climbed in, slithering into the water until it came up to her neck. "Oh, this feels grand, simply grand." She closed her eyes and leaned back against the curved, porcelain rim, luxuriating in it.

"Percy, I'm sorry about what happened earlier. It won't happen again, I swear."

"Forget it," Percy murmured, eyes still closed. "Besides, I've been a little rough on Lily. You were just trying to be nice to her, sort of level out the playing field."

They shared a moment's silence, the warm scent of the lavender relaxing both women.

"Percy, do you mind if I say something?"

"Say anything you like," Percy replied in a drowsy tone.

"I think you're rougher on *yourself* than anybody else." She rushed on, "I mean, you're always so down on yourself for your looks and your weight and your height when really, if you'd look at yourself the way a lot of other people do, like right now…"

Percy opened her eyes and turned to her younger sister folding and unfolding her wet clothes by the hamper. "Right now? I'm naked, for crying out loud."

"Exactly! You look like that picture. You know, that lady with the long hair standing on the half-shell coming out of the water. She's holding her long, red hair in front of her, you know, over her private parts."

Percy stared at her.

Sera went on, "The painting, you know, the old one, over in Europe somewhere." She thought for a moment. "Gee, I hope it doesn't get blown up in the war or something. I sure like that picture." She looked back at Percy. "You got to know who I mean. She looks regal and all that kind of stuff, like you do sometimes. It's almost like that famous guy painted you. I saw it once it in Life Magazine. The painting." Frustrated, Sera exploded. "What are you, a simpleton? The painting!"

Percy struggled to think, as she sat upright. "You mean 'Venus Rising From the Sea' by Botticelli?"

"Bingo! That's it. Only I call it Venus on the half shell. I looked at it for a long time, too. I said to myself --"

"I said, self," Percy interjected, imitating Sera's voice. "My sister, Percy, looks just like that broad in the painting, only without the shell."

"Yeah, that's what I said. You can make fun all you want, Persephone Cole, but you looked enough like her to make me remember it. Not that I particularly watch you taking a bath or nothing - I got better things to do -- but I have seen you in the altogether from time to time. Like tonight," Sera added.

"You can't share a bathroom with this family without seeing a lot of each other, that's true," Percy said, stifling a laugh. "Well, thank you, Serendipity. That's really sweet of you. You're good for my ego. Maybe I should get a copy of that picture, hang it up here in the bathroom. Better idea, maybe I should hang around my family a lot more." She laughed and leaned back again in the warm water, wiggling her toes tentatively. "My toes seem to be working again."

"Speaking of hanging around with the family, Percy, can I ask you something? Advice?"

"Of course. Hand me the soap, would you?"

Sera grabbed a bar of soap from the sink and tossed it to Percy before speaking. "Sammy's asked me to marry him."

Percy stopped lathering her hands and stared at her younger sister. "Sammy, the baker?" Sera nodded. "Sammy asked you to marry him?" Sera nodded again, but this time looked down. "Do you love him?" Sera shrugged her shoulders and didn't look up. "Sera, look at me. Look at me." Sera obeyed, her eyes brimming with tears. Percy studied her sister's lovely face, youthful and hopeful. "I can see you don't," Percy whispered.

"I'm scared, Percy. I don't want to wait forever. Maybe he's the only guy who'll ask me."

"First of all, Sera, he's not going to be the only guy to ask you. You'll have dozens." Percy said in a stronger voice, "And second, but more important, marriage is tough enough when both people love each other so much they're going to pop with it. If you're ambivalent, you don't stand a chance."

"What's 'ambivalent'?"

"Wishy-washy."

"What about you and Leo? Didn't you love him until you thought you would 'pop'? Look what happened. You got screwed."

"Hey," Percy said, throwing the washcloth at her. "I said *both* people. How did I know Leo was a louse? My libido had taken over. And don't ask me to explain that word to you, 'cause I won't. It was the right feelings I had. The right feelings. But for the wrong guy. Now give me back my washcloth."

Sera tossed the cloth back. "Gee, this is fun. We haven't talked like this since….I can't remember. Months even."

"We will more often, Sera. I promise. But no more talk about marrying Sammy or any other guy for at least a year or two. You're barely twenty. You got time."

"Well, I don't want to wind up as old as you were. We thought you'd never get married! I mean you were an old maid – ancient -- for crying out loud."

Percy took a deep breath. "Girlie chat is over. Go away," she said, as she slipped under the water and out of sight.

* * * *

Two hours later, Percy turned from the girl at the stove, took her plate to the table and began to fill it from the mound of French toast steaming on a large platter.

"Now that we're alone, Lily, I want to ask you a couple of questions."

Lily let out a resigned sigh, took off her apron and sat down primly across the table from Percy. She stared at her expectantly. "Yes, Miss Cole?"

Before answering, Percy spread butter on the three pieces of egg-soaked, fried toast and poured on the maple syrup. She knew her mother had been saving the syrup for at least two years waiting for a 'special occasion.' Had she known the special occasion was French toast, she might have tried her hand at making up some herself.

"Lily, what time were you and Connie finished working at Santa Land the night he was killed?"

Lily looked slightly startled, as if this was the last question in the world she expected to hear. "Let me see. It seems so long ago." She thought for a minute. "Eight-thirty. Yes, that's it, eight-thirty. Santa Land closes at eight, and we left about thirty minutes later. Why?"

Percy chewed a large mouthful of French toast, butter and syrup and closed her eyes appreciatively. She didn't answer Lily's question but said,

"This is the best French toast I've ever had. What the hell did you put in it?"

Getting used to Percy's ways, Lily smiled before answering. "A little vanilla, a half a teaspoon of cinnamon, and a sprinkle of nutmeg. Your mother had everything in the kitchen. The spices are a little old but still serviceable."

"You'd never know anything in this kitchen was serviceable." Percy waggled a forkful of the food in front of Lily. "You should open a restaurant, kiddo. I mean it. You are one grand cook."

"Thank you," Lily murmured.

"So what did you do between eight-thirty and two-thirty, before you both showed up at your father's store?"

"What did we do?" Lily echoed, her face set in thought and puzzlement. "We went back to my apartment at Beekman Place. Yes, that's what we did."

"All that time?" Percy shoveled another forkful of dripping toast in her mouth but studied Lily's face.

"Sure, all that time. We sat around, had some laughs, a few drinks. Oh, yes. I made us some tuna fish sandwiches. Connie liked my tuna fish sandwich. I use fresh dill. Grandfather doesn't though. I made his plain with dill pickles."

"Who else was there, besides your grandfather?" Percy finished the last of the French toast, wiped her mouth on a napkin and stood, looking down at Lily.

"Well, Hanson. Hanson's always there. He's the butler. He doesn't have anybody else except us. He's been with the family for over forty years. Everybody else comes in daily, even the cook."

"What's her name?"

"I don't know. She's new. I just call her cook. She's gone by six or seven. If anyone's ever home at dinner time, Hanson reheats, serves and clears."

"Did you make him a tuna fish sandwich?"

Lily bristled. "You don't do that with Hanson. He's far too formal. I left enough in the refrigerator, in case he wanted some, but he never does."

"You don't like Hanson?"

"Hanson doesn't like me. Or my father." She let out a self-deprecating laugh. "He puts up with us. He's devoted to Grandfather." After a beat of silence, she asked, "What is it?"

"What?"

"You had an expression on your face I'd never seen before."

"I was thinking for the first time, Lily, you *are* a poor little rich girl."

Percy started for the door, but turned back. "Lily, you'd better put your wanderlust aside and stay locked in the apartment no matter what. I'm not trying to scare you – well, yes, I am. Danny DeLuca broke out of jail a couple of days ago." Something told her not to mention the car incident of a few hours ago.

Was that DeLuca? Could have been. I was too busy spinning on the hood of a car to tell.

Lily leapt up and backed away, only stopping when she bumped into the stove. "Do you think he knows…" The sound of her voice petered out. She looked lost in thought. Her eyes had a far-away, frightened look in them.

Percy snapped her fingers several times to get the girl's attention. "Where you are? Come back, come back, wherever you are," she sang out.

Lily's head snapped around; her eyes became focused on Percy. "Sorry."

"In answer to your question, I don't know yet. I plan to find out more today. You can't stay here if DeLuca does know and he's out there. I've got Oliver to think of. I don't want him caught in the middle of --"

"Of course, not," Lily jumped in. "I should leave. I should leave right away. I've stayed too long. I don't want anybody hurt because of me."

"Hold on. Don't panic and don't do anything rash. Let me see what's what. I'll know more later. Promise me you'll stay put until I find some things out."

Lily nodded, unhappy. She looked up at Percy.

"I promise."

Chapter Eighteen

After putting on a pair of her brother's old hiking boots from the back of the hall closet, Percy was able to walk, swollen toes and all, with not much of a limp. At nine a.m. she walked instead of hobbled into the jewelry shop and found it going full force. She looked around at what she considered to be the crime scene.

Busy behind the counter making sales and handling sparkling baubles, were Mr. Waller, Miss Lorner, and an elderly gentleman she'd never seen before. All three were smiling the salesman smile as they waited on several harried people, three men and one woman. They answered questions in a subservient but superior way, something that can only be done when the other guy may be the one with the dough but you're the one with the smarts.

I guess rich folks throwing their big bucks away at Christmas time need help just like the rest of us poor slobs.

Percy waited to the side near a lone, uncomfortable looking, white satin chair. She took the opportunity to study each of the three sales people individually. Possibly in honor of the holiday season, Janice Lorner wore a bright red knit dress stretched tightly over her curvaceous figure. Again, no jewelry or makeup adorned her. Black-rimmed reading glasses emphasized her librarian looks from the neck up, especially with the tight bun at the back of her head.

Percy's eyes traveled to the white-haired man fawning over the lone female customer. Bearing a family resemblance to the younger man, she surmised the elderly one to be Lily's grandfather. His hands shook a little, but other than that, he

stood erect and retained the polished aura of a successful businessman. His smile, while seemingly genuine on one level, was a little too bright and constant for Percy's taste. He'd given her the once over when she entered the shop and she'd noticed his sharp, observing eyes. This was a man who didn't miss much.

While considerable taller than his father, William Waller remained stooped over, carrying a 'dowager's hump' on his back, something Percy accredited to much older people, as a rule. Percy realized he was only about ten years older than herself, maybe his mid-forties, yet his demeanor was that of a much older man. His receding hairline didn't help, even though what sparse hair toughing it out was nearly jet black in color.

Speaking of balding heads, she thought, *I'd better go see what Harry knows about the Christmas angel's death. Too bad I didn't bring my baseball bat. I could have used it to field off his passes.*

She stepped to the other side of the chair and let three men pass her by, each one holding a small lavender and white paper bag containing a wrapped present. There were going to be three happy women come Christmas morning, judging by these men's expressions. Each one looked like the cat that swallowed the canary.

I bet you get a lot of yeses with diamonds.

The middle-aged woman gathered a long, sleek black fur coat around her and exited empty handed, followed by a young man wearing a grin on his face. The grin was probably due to the diamond encrusted watch Percy saw him clamp on his wrist moments after the older woman forked over a check.

Her son? Her lover? Who cares?

The store momentarily devoid of customers, Percy stepped forward to the main counter. "Good morning." She kept her voice respectful but commanding.

Both William Waller and Miss Lorner smiled half-heartedly and moved toward her. The elder Waller stepped back. He glared at Percy like an eagle eyeing a small mouse from aloft, promising to pounce when least expected. She kept her gaze on him, as well, mindful she was looking down on a much smaller human being. He looked tired, but here was a man aware of positions of power, she surmised. She would try to use her height to advantage.

"You must be the senior Mr. Waller," she said extending her hand. After a slight hesitation, he took her hand in his and shook it. But his glare, almost rude, did not change.

"I'm Persephone Cole. I've been hired --"

"I know who you are," he interrupted with a voice larger than she expected, while dropping her hand. "My son foolishly asked you to help Lily, who is beyond help, in my opinion."

He turned to the other woman. "Miss Lorner, why don't you take your break now? We are experiencing a lull in clientele."

"Of course, Mr. Waller," she said demurely, with a nod of the head and nearly curtsying. She grabbed a small purse and folded coat from behind the counter and, without putting the coat on, hurried out the door before anyone could say anything.

Percy was stunned at the other woman's obsequious behavior. The younger Waller watched the woman leave. As the door to the shop closed behind his clerk and paramour, he turned to his father.

"Now, Dad, Lily is not --" William Waller began, but was cut off by the older man.

"William, I have told you repeatedly, that girl is no better than her mother was."

"Please," William Waller said, his only word on the subject. His voice had a futile edge to it, as if he had heard this many times before and would hear it many times again.

"A pretty damning statement, Mr. Waller," Percy said to the old man. "Care to explain it?"

"I do not." His words were clipped and his voice cold. "Other than to say your services are no longer required. Please leave these premises." He stared up at her, his expression unyielding.

"I don't think so, bub," Percy replied, crossing her arms across her chest. "You didn't hire me and you can't fire me." She turned to William Waller. "You firing me, Mr. Waller?"

Waller didn't reply but shook his head. He turned away from the counter and headed to the back room. Percy followed. Glancing back, she saw the senior Waller remained poised and stiff, almost like a statue, burning eyes flitting from one person to the other, as they left the room.

Waller shut his office door and crumpled into his chair like a beaten down man. "You'll have to excuse my father, Miss Cole. He's not a well man, for all his ranting. He has a weak heart."

"Bad ticker, Huh? I didn't realize that was license to act like a son of a bitch."

Waller stiffened. "I'd like to remind you it's my father you're talking about."

"I'd like to remind you, it's your daughter *he's* talking about. And she's in serious trouble. You know about the second murder last night?"

Waller nodded, with a head so low it almost laid on his chest. He looked about to burst into tears.

"Oh, God," He said and rubbed a hand over a too quickly shaven face, patches of stubble and a nick on the chin revealing the truth. "Did she do it? I don't know, anymore."

"Well, I do. She didn't. Lily's probably guilty of a lot of things, but murder isn't one of them. Where were you night before last, mister? How do you account for yourself?"

"I don't have to--" He broke off, shaking his head.

"Yeah, you do. I found out something interesting. Gracie Mansion is only a ten-minute drive from here at that time of night. These are little bits of info cops are only too glad to pass along. And you say you have an iron-clad alibi but I read a detailed police report that states you left the table for about an hour during the poker game."

"I took a nap in one of the bedrooms," he retorted, spittle landing on his chin. "Everybody does that at marathon poker games."

"Nobody remembers seeing you during that time. Very convenient, that. Maybe you weren't there when you said you were. People say a lot of things."

I'm making that last part up, buster, but one thing about marathon poker games, nobody can keep track of everybody all the time.

"That's ridiculous," Waller practically yelled. "All the players were going in and out of the poker room, about fifteen of us. How could somebody not see me? Everybody saw everybody."

"So you say. An hour would give you plenty of time to sneak out, drive here, shoot the elf, and drive back."

His face registered shock and dismay. "How *dare* you imply that I would --"

"Again with this imply thing?" She drew herself up as tall as she could and looked down at him. "Don't you people know anything? Imply means to hint at. Infer means to state implicitly. I'm not hinting, buster, I'm saying it outright. You *could* have left the game, driven here and shot Connie. Maybe you didn't, but you could have." She leaned over him. "Why doesn't Lily like you? I can see why she doesn't like the old man; he's a pip. But you? I don't get it."

He wriggled in his chair, discomfort outweighing embarrassment. "I don't know." He looked imploringly at Percy. "Her mother and I weren't getting along at the time of her death. It had been a bad marriage. The only thing good about it was Lily. I love Lily, as if she were my own --"

"Wait a minute," Percy interrupted. "What do you mean, as if she were your own? You mean she's not your daughter?"

"Lily was two-years old when Verna and I married. I adopted her and she is my daughter, in the eyes of the law and in mine." He stuck his chin out defiantly, as if daring Percy to challenge him.

"She knows she's adopted, right? I mean, I can't imagine someone like your father letting that tidbit go."

"Of course, she does. As for my father, he's never forgiven me for marrying Verna and not having children of my own. He thinks I've let him down. Maybe I have. Lily, too. I've tried my best with her. I loved her mother. Verna's the one who cheated on me. I was always there for her, always. I tried to shield Lily from all the sordid details. Maybe that was a mistake. She thinks I...I don't know what she thinks." He sucked in a deep breath. Even though he'd stopped speaking, his eyes continued to tell a story of betrayal, misunderstanding, and pain.

"You never talked to Lily about this?" He shook his head. "What are you, a moron? No wonder she's a nutcase. Does she at least know you and her mother were having problems?"

"I don't know. Maybe, yes." He rallied, his voice gaining strength and certainty. "How can she not know? She was there."

"Maybe because she was just a kid. She was busy learning how to tie her shoes, not keeping track of what the adults were doing. Jesus, I thought my family was odd. You beat us by a mile."

He reached out a shaky hand and poured water from the glass tumbler into a glass. "You know, this is really none of your business. You're job is to shield Lily. I hired you to--"

"Yeah, yeah, to find out who killed the elf," Percy interrupted. "And now who killed the Christmas angel. And possibly to keep Lily from spending time in jail, unlike Danny Deluca -- who by the way -- flew the coop, so he could have killed either of them or both. You know, Mr. Waller, I think there's a lot of shielding going on around here. Maybe Lily should come forward and take her lumps like the rest of us Joe Blows." She monitored his reaction.

What are you going to say now, bub? You going to throw Lily to the lions the way your father would?

A look of horror struck the jeweler's face and he put down the glass of water with a clunk. "No, no. Don't say that, please. She's afraid of enclosed places. Tell me she's safe."

"She's safe, for now. But if I keep your daughter out of jail, you owe me five thousand bucks. I got a piece of paper right here that says so." She tapped the breast pocket of her jacket.

He sat up straighter in the chair. "I am a man of my word."

"That's good to know."

"There's something else," he said, his voice tentative and soft. He began to play with one of the empty jewelry cases on his desk again, the way he had the first time Percy interviewed him. She sat down, opened her mouth to speak, but waited.

"We were robbed again. Oh, not much, just some little earrings shaped like a cross, seed pearls and diamond chips, hardly worth three hundred dollars, but I thought I should mention it."

"What do you mean, 'again'?

Waller seemed nervous and spoke in a rushed, almost a guilty tone. "The day after the ...ah...elf was found in the store window, I noticed one of my diamond solitaires was missing, a smaller one, probably worth seven or eight hundred dollars.

I was so busy with the murder and all, I didn't notice it until the next day."

"Go on."

He cleared his throat. "The funny thing is," he said, leaning forward, "Both robberies didn't set the alarms off and I've found no evidence of a break in. I had to recheck my stock inventory to make sure I hadn't miscounted."

"And had you?"

"No. Miss Lorner and I did it together. Every piece is accounted for except those two. They were here and now they're gone." He shuddered and sank down in his chair. "I'd hate to think Lily…although they were inexpensive, comparatively."

"That's sad," Percy said, in a voice devoid of emotion.

"What?" he turned to her with a questioning look on his face.

"That she's the person who comes to your mind. I think if Lily took the jewelry, Mr. Waller," Percy said in a voice sharper than she meant, "She would have taken two of the larger pieces in the house. That's what I would have done."

He let out a soulful laugh. "Anyway, their disappearance is a mystery to me, especially as I test the alarms every day."

"And they work fine?"

He didn't reply but nodded, a sad, wistful look coming into his eyes.

"You going to report the thefts?"

He gave a small shake of his head.

"Still not convinced it wasn't Lily?" He didn't reply. "If that's all, Mr. Waller, I'll get going." She turned to leave, but paused and looked back at the man huddled in his office chair, a man who still wasn't spilling everything he knew.

"And take it easy. You look like a man who's lost his best friend."

* * * *

"Business don't look so good out there, Harry. I guess a couple of murders put a crimp in Christmas at Santa Land." She walked inside the small office, closing the door behind her.

"Oy! You again," Harry said, pivoting in his chair to face her. "Okay, Red, what do you want? Isn't it bad enough my business is dying?"

"Like a lot of people around here. The only little kiddies showing up come with armed guards?"

"Something like that. Leave it to the newspapers to slaughter me. Now I'll never make any profit."

"Poor you." Percy couldn't help but laugh at the self-absorption of the man.

"Yeah, January in Palm Beach is out this year. Happy? Now get out." Harry turned back to his littered desk and threw a pencil in the corner in frustration.

"Aw gee, Harry. And here I thought you'd be glad to see me. Where's the dog?" She looked down at the empty dog basket.

"He's out for a walk, if it's any of your business, which it ain't." His voice was gruff.

"Everybody's telling me to mind my own business. I must be doing something right."

Percy's light-hearted banter stopped. Uninvited, she plopped down in the chair to the left of the desk and leaned in to Harry. She picked up the five by seven photo of him, his wife and a teenage boy and wiped off what looked like years of fingerprints. "I want to talk to you about Gertie."

"What about her? She's dead." His words were flippant but Percy noted a slight shake in his voice at the end. He snatched at the framed photo, his hands shaking even more than his voice.

"Why so nervous, Harry?"

"What do you think, Red? It's like someone's out to get me."

"If they were out to get you, they'd have bumped you off, not everybody else in a Christmas costume."

He looked startled at first then fear took over.

"Don't look so scared," she said. "Tell me what you're not telling me. Maybe I can help you."

He shook his head, white speckled eyebrows fluttering up and down nervously.

"What was Gertie doing here after hours, almost at midnight? Pretty late hours to be working."

He shook his head again, still not saying a word. He wouldn't look at Percy. She pressed on.

"Don't you count heads before you lock up? How'd she get left behind?"

"Gertie's got her own set of keys," he finally said, then corrected himself. "Had her own set of keys. She's been working for me for thirteen years. Why shouldn't she have her own set of keys?" Harry looked up for the first time, his tone belligerent.

"No reason, Harry. Calm down. I'm here to help you," she drawled.

He let out a knowing chuckle. "Yeah, help me, right. You're going to help me right into the poor house, along with…"

"Along with who, Harry?" Percy asked after a moment, fixing a hard stare on the man. "Gertie stayed here in this building, didn't she? Everybody left, but she stayed here and met someone. Maybe she let someone in; maybe they were already here."

The fear on Harry's face was replaced by terror.

"Someone who killed her." Percy pushed on. "Maybe blackmail? What's going on around here, Harry? Who owns this building? And who's walking your dog, Harry? Who's walking your dog?"

Harry jumped up with such force, his chair pushed back and slid across the cement floor with a loud screech. His drew himself up to his full five foot six inch height.

"Get out," he commanded and pointed to the door.

"Nice try. You don't look like you could pull off an 'or else' kind of threat, but I appreciate the bluster." Percy put down the framed photograph, rose slowly and moved forward on the man. He backed up instinctively. "You know, you're lucky I don't smack you one, just on general principles."

Harry swallowed a retort and crossed to the door, not looking at the larger woman. "Get out now or I'll call the police and have you charged with trespassing."

"Why don't you do that, Harry?" The fear returned to the man's face. "Don't worry. I'm going."

She let out a chortle and strolled to the door. Harry opened the door and pulled his body as far back from her as he could. She stepped over the threshold, but turned back to face the man.

"I guess this means drinks tonight are off, huh, Harry? Aw, gee, and here I thought we were getting to be such good friends." He slammed the door in her face.

Percy dropped the smirk on her face. Her body lost its casual swagger and became tense, nearly rigid. With quiet steps, she hurried up and down the hallway opening and

closing doors. She came to one with an older hinged hasp that couldn't be opened, wearing a fairly new lock. A check in either direction told her no one was around, although she could hear general noise coming from the other side of the double doors leading to Santa Land. One quick look at the

rusty hasp told her it could be broken easily. She removed a short, thick screwdriver from her jacket, one carried there for purposes such as these.

With one strong thrust, she jabbed it in between the door and the hinge and rocked the screwdriver back and forth. Rusted screws broke free of their wooden imprisonment with a minimum of effort and the hinge pulled free of the door. It took less than ten seconds. Another quick glance to make sure no one saw her, and she pushed the door open to reveal uneven, cement stairs heading down, down, down into darkness.

She put the screwdriver back into her breast pocket, withdrew a small flashlight from another, and turned it on. Percy took two steps down then reached back and closed the door behind her. Aiming the shaft of light on each narrow tread of the staircase, she descended one ginger step at a time.

Half way down, she discovered a light switch on the wall and struck at it with the palm of her hand. A low-watt naked light bulb, hanging down on a frayed cord from the cement ceiling below, spurted on. She continued downward, her feet crunching on dirt, pebbles and pulverized cement granules, her nose twitching at decades of stagnant air.

What the hell kind of place is this? It looks like it's the center of the earth or something Jeesh, what a maze. Where do these passageways lead off to, I wonder? Brrr! It's colder than a witch's tit down here. And the word depressing takes on a new meaning. As Bette Davis says, 'What a dump.'

The beam of her flashlight scanned more of the darkness below and found a battered chair, small table, and reading lamp in one corner. Percy continued down the stairs and moved toward the lone grouping in the room. Hesitating, but not sure why, she yanked on the pull chain of the table light. The small, cramped area was suffused in a warm glow. Percy, always aware of battery usage, turned off the flashlight and returned it to her pocket. A neatly taped, nineteen forty-two calendar hung on the wall behind the table, the white and

black of its pages standing out against the dull, grey cement.

'X's covered the days of the current month, with December thirty-first encircled in bright red several times. She shuffled through the pages of the calendar, starting from the beginning. Each month had the days 'X'd out.

Uneasy, Percy backed up, about to turn and leave when she noticed something even more peculiar. Above the pitiful arrangement, a once transparent glass window was blackened out by layers of dark-colored paint. It had also been taped shut. Outside light and fresh air were not welcomed here.

Percy puzzled over what kind of a person would lay claim to this deed and, deep in thought, heard the sound too late to do anything. It came short and fast, more like a whoosh, and then she felt the crack on the side of her head. It was followed by a sharp intake of breath, probably hers, the yip of a small dog, and the hard cement floor rising up to meet her falling body.

Chapter Nineteen

"Who does she think she is, this fat, nosy, busy-body? I knew she'd come snooping around here. I knew it." He huffed, pushing her dead weight over and tying the ropes tight around Percy's wrists. "What am I going to do with her? She'll ruin everything. I can't let her ruin everything."

His face grimaced and a flood of tears filled his eyes. The dog, nervous and shaking, began to whimper. The man took his anger out on the dog.

"Shut up, you!" The dog, tail between his legs ran into a corner of the dimly lit room. The man felt bad. "I'm sorry, boy. I'm sorry."

He turned and looked at the unconscious woman at his feet. "What am I going to do with you?" He paced back and forth for a moment.

Percy began to moan.

"Oh, God! She's coming to. What'll I do? Papa! Papa will know." He turned to leave, the dog began to follow. "No, no, boy! You stay here. You watch her, boy. Stay!" The dog obeyed and sat, confused and anxious, tongue lolling to the side as he panted heavily staring at the inert woman.

Chapter Twenty

Percy opened her eyes with difficulty. She was first aware of the cold, hardness of the cement floor, then the stale, stuffy air. She tried to move, get more comfortable, but her bound hands behind her back prevented her from doing so. Her head pounded on the left side and her right cheek, the one on which she'd fallen, burned and ached.

"What the…what happened? She said aloud.

The dog let out a yelp in answer and began to whine. Percy tried to focus her eyes and saw the small brown dog sitting about fifteen feet away. He rose and started to move closer but hesitated and began to trot back and forth, uneasy and frightened.

Take a number, kiddo. I'm a little scared about what's going on around here, myself.

Percy struggled to sit up. Sitting with one leg behind her, she was glad whoever did this to her had neglected to turn the light off on the small table.

"Well, this isn't very comfy." She looked at the dog. "And you don't look any happier than me." The dog gave out a short bark but stayed his ground.

Percy strained at the ropes on her wrists. They were tight, biting into her skin with every move.

"Where's your master, boy? Gone off somewhere planning to come back and finish me off?" The dog whined but wagged his tail tentatively. "So you say. Well, if you were any kind of dog, you'd be like Lassie and get me out of this mess. Wait a minute, the knot feels looser, bigger than it should be. I don't think your master did such a great job of tying me up." She yanked her wrists apart as much as she could in several painful jerks, trying to ignore what the rough hemp was doing to her flesh.

Curious at her movements, the dog inched his way closer and sniffed the air, as if for clues on what was going on.

"If I can just get my hands free, doggy," she muttered, pushing and pulling at the ropes behind her, "Maybe I can get at the screwdriver, which is a pretty good weapon, if he left it in my pocket. That is, if he doesn't have a gun. He have a gun, doggy?"

She'd continued to talk to the dog. It helped to lessen the pain in her torn wrists and hands. Finally, Percy scrunched her bloodied and scraped right hand free of its bindings followed by her left hand. She withdrew a small hanky from her pocket and dabbed at the blood with shaky fingers.

The dog came up to her, half crawling, tail dragging on the floor. She reached out and stroked it on the head. "You looked more scared than me, doggy. You're a funny looking thing, with those short legs and long body. And what's with the scruffy hair? But I'll bet you're a good dog."

The dog's attention left her. He cocked his head upward, ears alert, as if he heard something overhead. Percy, too, though she heard a sound above, the click of a door, possibly the sound of footfall. Her eyes scanned the low ceiling and rested on the staircase in the corner. She reached inside her jacket pocket, aware of how stiff and swollen her right hand had become, and felt for the screwdriver.

What about the flashlight? She felt that, too, right where she'd put it. Fighting off the desire to lie down with the oncoming headache, Percy struggled to her feet. Trembling hands grappled at freeing the flashlight in her pocket. All the while her mind raced.

I'm amazed. If I cracked somebody over the head and tied them up, I'd make damned sure there was nothing they could use as a weapon on them. This guy must be a real amateur. Or maybe he got interrupted. Whatever, I need to get out of here before he comes back, maybe to finish the job.

Percy aimed the search light at the walls for an exit other than the staircase and found a small entrance to a tunnel in each of the three walls.

Leading to God knows where, but any place is better than here.

Percy eeny, meeny, miney, moed and chose the tunnel 'mo' landed on. Feeling a little more secure on her feet, she started for it. The funny looking dog made a faint move to follow her then hesitated. Percy stepped forward and faced the small creature that drew back in alarm.

"Easy, boy. Take it easy. You want to come with me?" Her voice was gentle. "Well, why not? Seems like you've got a raw deal down here. Come on, doggy," she called, as she went through the narrow entrance into a low ceilinged passageway. The dog's ears perked up and he scampered behind into the looming blackness then dashing ahead to take the lead. She listened to the pitter-patter of his feet, following its sound.

"You look like you know where you're going, doggy. I'm glad one of us does."

Mindful of the low ceiling, she stooped over a bit. Dampness and stagnant air assaulted her nose, far worse than the room she'd been in. Percy fought off nausea and looked back to make sure they weren't being followed by her unknown assailant.

Straining her eyes, she shot the beam of light into the tunnel. It was clear as far as she could see. There were several smaller tunnels off to the right of this main one, some with doors, some without. Further inside, Percy heard hollow whistles of air being pulled in and around. Drafts of cold air curled around her ankles and feet. It didn't help the smell or the dampness, either. Percy shivered and wished, once again, she's worn her overcoat.

You got to learn how to dress, toots.

She kept the dog under close surveillance, comforted by his seeming knowledge of where he was going. He'd obviously traversed these tunnels many times.

And lived to tell the tale. Or should I say, tail? She grimaced. *I shouldn't make puns. They're bad for the mind.*

She stopped at the first offshoot of the tunnel, a plywood door, all the while keeping a running monolog directed to the dog that pattered back to her and stayed close.

"You know about the depths of Manhattan, doggy? It's like Swiss cheese under the sidewalks and buildings. New York City's got more underground tunnels, subways, burrows, and who knows what beneath the streets than any other city in the world. I take that back. Maybe Paris has more, huh, doggy? I forgot about the sewers of Paris. But we got sewers here, too. You ever read *Phantom of the Opera*? Written by a French guy, Gaston Leroux? No, I suppose not. You don't look like the intellectual type."

She pushed open the door and threw a beam of light into what appeared to be a room instead of another tunnel. The room was stuffed with overturned boxes, trash and extraneous lumber. It, too, had a blacked out window.

"Seems someone's taking the war effort to extreme." She looked down at the dog sitting at her feet. "Or maybe someone's hiding something from prying eyes. What do you think, doggy?" She flashed the light down on the scruffy, panting dog that eyed her with curiosity, as they both stood in the tunnel outside the strange room. "You're not saying, eh? Well, you have to learn to keep up your end of the conversation." She turned around and faced where she came from, shooting a beam of light into the blackness.

"I don't see anyone coming after us yet. You bark if you hear someone, okay?" The dog, happy with this attention sneezed, wagging his tail.

"Okay, let's keep looking for a way out. I'm not heading back, if I can help it." Percy closed the door and pressed forward. The dog raced on ahead, almost as if he knew the way out. Percy picked up speed until she came to another door, this one larger and sturdier than the previous one. She pushed at the door, which scraped along the uneven cement floor. The room was warmer, much warmer than the tunnel. A faint, reddish glow came from the center of the room. It took Percy a split second to realize it was a large, freestanding furnace. A thick pipe shot up on an angle, into a corner of the ceiling above. The warmth felt good and Percy stepped inside. A smartly made cot sat in a corner. Several throw pillows lined the back of the cot against the wall, creating a small couch. Butting the head of the cot was a small table, piled high with neatly stacked comic books on one end and hard cover books on the other. Sandwiched in the middle was a metal lamp with a lone bulb. She turned it on. The dim light cast long shadows. At the foot of the cot, a short bookshelf was crammed with regular books, as if waiting for the next choice of the reader. Drawn to this peculiar but homey oasis, Percy picked up one of the comic books from the square, non-descript table.

"Dick Tracy?" She spread the thick stack open like a fan. "Looks like there's every Dick Tracy comic book ever printed." She restored the order and snatched up one of the hard cover books, which looked much used.

"*The Hardy Boys, The House on the Cliff.* What the...?"

Percy picked up another book from the pile, a thick Webster's Dictionary, also worn with use. A third was a book on sailing, with many dog-eared pages. Puzzled, Percy went to the small bookshelf at the foot of the cot. A fast scan of the titles showed her more Hardy Boys and several books on

different hobbies, including a 'how to' on learning Morse Code. But it was the top shelf that most intrigued her. Here were several smaller, thin books, some covers pliant, some not, and in a variety of colors. Each had a year written on the binding, chronologically starting at nineteen thirty-one.

Got to be diaries or journals. They look like one I had back in the sixth grade.

Drawn to the current year, Percy pulled out the soft cover, black leather book and leafed through it. As she suspected, it was a journal. What she read on only a few of the pages made her want to get out of the basement as quickly as possible. Rolling it up to fit into her pocket, she crammed the book inside. She would study it in detail later.

I don't know what the hell is going on but I'm not waiting for that lunatic to find me again.

Aloud she said, "Let's keep searching, doggy, for another way out. She bent over and looked into his face. "Are you with me?" A thumping tail answered her question. On her way out of the room, she saw a large box of what looked like firecrackers against a far wall, as far away as possible from the heat of the furnace.

Is that whole box filled with firecrackers? If so, that's a lot of celebrating, even for the Fourth of July.

A quick examination of the deep box revealed it was, indeed, stuffed with firecrackers. Another puzzler. But Percy didn't have time to reason it out. She went back to the door and again shot a beam of light down the long tunnel from where she had just come. No one.

Where is this guy? He just knocks me out, ties me up, and takes a powder?

She touched the lump on her head, which was increasing in size.

I need some ice.

She felt the dog brush by her leg, as she stepped out into the main tunnel. The beam of her flashlight caught his

rump as the dog ran ahead, happier, more of a bounce to his step.

About one-hundred feet ahead, the dog ran up a short set of steps to the left, stopped and turned to her expectantly.

A way out!

Percy ran after the dog and stopped at the bottom of the four steps, out of breath.

"What did you find, doggy? Is this a way out? Holy crap, I hope so."

She went up the steps and looked for a handle on a thin but sturdy metal door. She found a knob but when she turned it, the locked door wouldn't budge. The door stood between Percy and freedom. She was about to bang on it, hoping someone would hear her on the other side, when she saw words crudely painted on the wall.

"'Watch repair.' Wait a minute. Is this the back end of Pierce's shop? That means the cobbler's shop should be a little bit back where we came from."

She jumped back down to the floor and retraced her steps some twenty feet. Sure enough, there she saw another set of steps leading up to another metal door. On the wall, printed crudely in red paint, was the word 'cobbler.' She turned the knob and struggled with this door, but it, too, seemed to be locked firmly on the other side. Once again, she hesitated on pounding on the door until she knew more. The sound might draw her attacker to right where she is, and after reading a few pages of his journal, that didn't appeal to her. Percy looked at her watch, difficult to read with the faint light reflecting on the crystal.

Six-thirty. I don't know if anyone will still be in these shops, even if I do bang on the door. Okay, don't panic. If the cobbler's shop is here and the watch repair is further down, does that mean Waller's jewelry shop is at the end of this tunnel? Well, why not? If not, you're screwed, Percy. You'll have to go back and face that Hardy Boy, yacht racing, Morse coding maniac to get out.

She focused the beam of light toward what she hoped was the path to Waller's store and noticed the dog still at the top step of the entrance to the watch repair shop. When he saw her looking at him, he gave a wiggle and a short bark.

"Ahhh. You want to go visit your little friend, Cougat? Sorry, kiddo. It's after closing and nobody's there. We've got to go on. So come on, boy. Come down from there," she said as she passed him. She heard the click of his nails on the wooden stairs as he descended. He scampered ahead, obviously looking on this adventure as a new game.

I'm glad someone's enjoying himself.

Continually casting light on both sides of the tunnel, she noticed she was trodding a slight incline. Soon there was less moisture on the walls and they seemed more finished, more care going into the workmanship. Ahead a beige brick wall delineated the two buildings joined at the bowels by this common tunnel. Percy passed through a doublewide passageway where the air became cleaner and more breathable. The dog hesitated for some reason.

"Come on, doggy. We've come this far. Don't crap out on me now." Nervous, the dog circled around, reluctant to go back and unwilling to go forward.

"Come here, you." Percy bent over and picked up the dog, who weighed more than she thought he would. "Hey, you're a hefty fella, aren't you? You must weight twenty, twenty-five pounds. My kinda guy." He began to pant heavily. "What's the matter with you? It's all right. You're going to be all right."

Carrying her new pal, she juggled the flashlight with the other hand. Percy continued walking the tunnel until she came to a set of stairs that ended at a door.

Chapter Twenty-one

"Well, this is it, kiddo. We're either making a bid for freedom here or we're going back." She set the dog down, so she'd have a free hand, but looked down and waggled a finger in his face.

"Don't you move, doggy. Stay. Stay." She said the last two words with emphasis then reached for the handle. The knob turned easily in her hand and the door opened inward on silent, well-oiled hinges. Her fingers felt for a possible light switch on the inside of the wall and found it. She flipped it on and was rewarded with a flood of light, blinding her until her eyes adjusted.

Another step up and she was inside an organized storage room, which held cardboard boxes filled with velvet jewelry cases of various sizes. Three glass display cases stood in the center of the room, one with a cracked top. Several tall metal lockers hugged a wall, each wearing a newish tumbler lock. At the end of the rectangular room was another set of steps leading up to a bigger door. After eye-balling the room for a second, she turned back to the dog that sat shivering on the other side of the door. Percy bent over and picked him up again.

"Okay, kiddo. I don't know what's got you so scared, but we're going to find out. So be a good boy, and stick with me. I'm kind of getting used to your company."

She closed the door to the tunnel behind her. After a pause, Percy pushed the sturdy-looking interior lock into its hold, noting the ease with which it slid in place. Had the door been locked from the inside, she would have never been able to get in.

"So why was it unlocked, kiddo?" She said to the dog in her arms. "Anybody from the tunnel can get in here." Her companion stopped panting and cocked his head at her, as if he was as surprised as she at the oversight. "Maybe that's the point."

"Let's go see if our luck's held and the other door is unlocked, as well."

Relieved to be out of the tunnel, she hopped up the steps and tried to the door. It was locked. This time she pounded and started to yell. The dog began to bark, as well.

"Hey! Hey! Anybody there? Let me out."

The dog continued to yip in unison, seemingly glad to be part of a new game.

She heard movement and the sounds of a lock being turned. She held the screwdriver in her hand as a weapon, not sure who was on the other side of the door. William Waller tentatively opened the door and looked from her to the dog in her arm in alarm. Percy concealed the unnoticed screwdriver in her sleeve and winked.

"Don't panic. It's only me." She bent over, deposited the dog on the floor, and straightened up.

The jeweler looked her up and down, shocked at her general dishevelment, and the soot and dirt clinging to her clothes. His eyes settled on her scratched cheek.

"Miss Cole! What the….How did you get in there? What happened to your face?"

"I came in through the tunnel into your storage room." She returned the screwdriver to her pocket. "As to what happened to my face, let's talk about that later. Can I use your sink to wash up?"

Thrown, he nodded mutely and pointed in a jerky manner. "Where did you say you came from? The storage room? I don't understand."

Percy didn't answer but pushed passed him, as did the dog that pranced ahead in the new game. Mr. Waller traipsed behind.

"Doesn't that dog belong to the owner of Santa Land?"

"No." Percy's reply was curt, as she turned on the hot water tap on the small bathroom sink. "You got any ice?"

"Ice?"

"Yeah, ice. I'd like to put it on this knot on my head. Somebody clobbered me a little while ago in the tunnel."

"Tunnel?"

"Yeah, tunnel. About that ice, Waller, you got any or not? I'm dying over here."

She began to wash her face with a nearby washcloth, concentrating on the abrasions on her hands and cheek. Once she cleaned up her face, the scratch was barely noticeable. The dog sat panting at her feet, watching the proceedings with great interest.

"You look like you could use some water, doggy." She picked up a large soap tray, clean and devoid of soap, and serviceable for her needs. She filled the tray with cool water and set it in front of the dog. He lapped loudly as he drank the water, finishing it off.

"You're a noisy fella," Percy observed. She refilled the tray with water and set it down again. The dog lapped again, this time leaving a small amount of water before he looked up at the woman expectantly. His eyes said, 'Okay, on to the next game.'

Waller watched for a moment then moved to a small refrigerator in his office. His hand reached absentmindedly for an ice pick lying on top of the appliance, as he spoke. "I would appreciate your telling me what's going on, Miss Cole."

"All in good time, Waller. Just get me that ice."

The jeweler shrugged and struck at a chunk of ice within the top freezer. Shards of ice fell into the lower tray. Looking around, but finding nothing, he pulled a large, white handkerchief from his pocket and began to fill it with chips of ice.

"I'm afraid I don't have an ice bag, Miss Cole."

She crossed over, took the handkerchief, and twisted the four ends of the cloth together. "This will do." With care, she held the hanky to the side of her head with the bruise. "Ahhh! That feels good. Now, I need your phone."

He nodded and gestured to the black upright sitting on his desk. She lifted the earpiece, set it on the desk, and dialed a memorized number with the same hand, as she slowly sat down. The other hand continued to hold the ice to her head. Percy picked up the earpiece again and listened, while saying, "Sit down, Mr. Waller. When I get through with this call, I need to ask a couple of questions." The other line answered and Percy leaned into the mouthpiece.

"Police Department? Yeah, is Detective Hutchers there? Good. Put me through. Tell him it's Percy Cole. I'll wait." She turned to Waller who sat and waited expectantly, much like the dog who had followed her into the office and sat at her feet.

"Who's running the store?" Her head gestured to the front of the jewelry shop.

"Janet is there. My father went home about thirty minutes ago. I close shop in about forty-five minutes."

Percy heard Hutchers' voice on the line. "Hey, I got something for you," she said into the mouthpiece. "He might fill your bill for the elf and angel murders."

"What?" Mr. Waller nearly leapt out of his chair. "Tell me!"

"Easy, boy," Percy said to the jeweler. "One step at a time." She spoke again into the phone. "If nothing else, Hutchers, I've got a good assault and battery charge to hang on him. That should make your day. Meet me over at Santa Land. How soon can you get there?" She listened. "Ten minutes? Nothing faster? Oh, all right. That gives me time to get the swelling down. I'll meet you there." She replaced the receiver on the hook.

"What's going on?" Waller sat upright in his chair and for the first time, made this an assertive question. "Tell me. I have a right to know."

"I'll ask the questions right now, if you don't mind. That's what you're paying me for." She moved the makeshift icepack around a little before staring at the middle-aged man. "Why was the storeroom door leading to the tunnels left unlocked?"

He leaned back in his chair and crossed one leg over the other. "The door leading to the tunnels was unlocked?"

"If you keep repeating everything I say, we're going to be here a long time. But I'll ask it again. Why would a storage room door, leading to a place where you keep very expensive baubles, be left unlocked and available to just about anybody on the block?"

"I have no idea what you're talking about."

She stared at the man long and hard. "How long has this business been here? Thirty years?"

"Forty."

"And you don't know the door on the other side of the storage room connects to a series of tunnels? What are you, a moron?"

He uncrossed his legs and leaned forward in anger. "Now see here, Miss Cole, that's the second time you've called me that and I don't appreciate --"

"Then stop acting like one and answer a simple question."

The jeweler wiggled around in his chair, ill at ease. He recrossed his legs and ran his finger along the precisely pressed seem along one leg of his slacks before he spoke, as if

needing the time to think. When he answered, his voice was so soft, Percy had to lean in to hear it.

"Actually, I do know about the tunnels and the door leading to them, but it's a very unpleasant memory. I never go near that door."

"Why, is it electrified or something?"

Percy let out a small laugh. Waller stared at her then cleared his throat.

"When I was a small child, I opened the door once, even though my father told me expressly not to. I went into the tunnel and the door closed behind me accidentally. It was pitch black. I was terrified, and began to scream. I must have been in there for over an hour, shrieking. I'll never forget it. My father finally rescued me then spanked me soundly for disobeying him. He placed the lock at a higher position so I couldn't reach it."

"You can reach it now."

He went on as if Percy hadn't spoken. "To my knowledge, the door has been locked ever since."

"No, it hasn't. It was open right now. I just came in that way."

Waller shrugged. "I wouldn't know. I'm rarely in the supply room, if that's what you mean."

"That's not exactly what I mean, but let's let it go." Her voice, harsh and clipped, lightened with the next statement. "You're quite an obedient son." She gave him a genuine smile. "Oliver would have gone back the next day to check out that tunnel, but he would have brought a flashlight with him."

"I'm not an aggressive character."

She studied him for a moment. "No, you're not." She stood up and handed him the dripping handkerchief containing the melting ice. "Thanks. My bump feels a lot better. I'll see you shortly, Waller." Percy moved for the door, followed by the dog.

He leapt up, trying to keep pace with her. "Don't you have an update to give me? I heard you tell the detective you may have found the killer."

"Possibly. I'll give you a full report later."

He scurried after Percy, still asking questions. "How's my daughter? How's Lily?"

"She's fine." Percy turned and faced him. "Look, I'll have something to tell you soon, Waller. I promise. First I need to clear up a few things."

Waller's eyes went to the dog at her feet. "You're sure that's not the man's dog from Santa --"

"No, it's not," Percy interrupted with finality. "But I am going to ask you to hold on to him for a few minutes. Think you can do that?"

"Well, I suppose I could lock him in the office. He's house trained, isn't he?"

Percy looked down at the dog that waited patiently at her feet. "You bet. He's a good dog." She squatted down. "Listen, doggy, you stay here. I'll be right back. Stay. Now you stay." The dog sat, cocked his head, but didn't move. "I wish everybody else paid attention to me the way this dog does."

Chapter Twenty-two

Hutchers got out of the unmarked, black police car and slammed the door in annoyance. "You better know what you're talking about, Perce. I broke several laws to get here in less than ten minutes."

"Get a speeding ticket, Hutchers? If you did, I might be able to get that fixed for you. I know somebody in high places."

"Very funny. So what gives?" He looked first at Percy then at the two uniformed policemen who tumbled out of the car, as well. "What are we doing here?"

"Come with me," Percy said, opening the front door of Santa Land. "I'll explain on the way."

She hurried past the throngs of noisy children, followed by Hutchers and the cops. Once back in the corridor, she threw open the office door to Harry's office and barged inside.

Harry was standing in the center of the room having an intense conversation with a shorter man in his early thirties, who was wearing what appeared to be thick, dark prescription glasses. The slight man was leaning into the older one, his body shaking. Harry had one arm around him, when they both turned to the sound of the opening door. Neither said a word as the four people descended upon them, but stood frozen in place, guilt and fear written all over their faces.

"Hutchers, allow me to introduce you to Harry's son, Ernie. He lives down in the basement and patrols the tunnels. He cracked me on the head and tied me up down there. I've got the knot to prove it." She pointed to the side of her head. "Also, here's a little journal you might find interesting." She pulled the diary out of her pocket and offered it to the detective.

"That's mine," said Ernie, coming to life once he recognized the diary. "You have no right to read that. No right at all. Tell them, Papa. That's not right," he whined.

Ernie wrung his hands together but didn't make a move toward the detective. His speech was slow, with careful enunciation. As he spoke, his features and expressions were not quite normal, although it was difficult to pinpoint what the problem was.

"Shhh, son." Harry began to stroke his son on the arm, in an effort to sooth him. "Don't get upset. It's all right. It will be all right."

Hutchers glanced at a few pages of the journal. With a surprised look, he pointed to a paragraph on a page dog eared by Percy. "What's this? It says right here you killed the elf."

Harry stepped in front on his son in a protective manner. "He didn't kill anyone. It's just pretend. He plays games with himself. He tries to write like he reads in the comic books, like Dick Tracy, but he'd never really hurt anybody."

"Oh, yeah?" Percy rubbed her head. "He sure hurt me."

"You frightened him," Harry retorted. "He doesn't like anyone in his tunnels."

"Take off those dark glasses, mister." Hutchers pointed a finger at Ernie. "Let me see your eyes."

"Please don't ask him to do that." Harry put an arm around his son, his voice resonant with apprehension. "It's too bright in here. The light hurts him." He noticed the doubt on the detective's face. "You see, when he was born, something happened with the umbilical cord around the baby's neck and the doctor's say Ernest was 'oxygen deprived.' Then…then…they were so upset over that, the doctor accidentally put too much silver nitrate in the baby's eyes. They were severely burned. He can't look at the world the way the rest of us do."

"Take them off." Hutchers put the professional growl in his voice, ignoring Harry's protests, but his eyes showed a flicker of doubt.

Ernie removed the dark glasses, but kept his eyes closed.

"Open your peepers," Hutchers demanded. "And keep them that way."

Harry's son blinked a couple of times then strained to keep grotesque bulging eyeballs, red and dripping, open.

"My God," said Hutchers. "That's enough to make a killer out of anyone. Put those things back on. Okay, let's go. You're under arrest. Take him away." He turned to the two policemen at his side.

"No, no!" Harry wrapped his arms around his son. "He doesn't do any of those things he writes. He just reads too many detective stories. He couldn't hurt anybody."

"I'll bet that's what Mrs. Capone says about her baby, Al," Percy remarked.

"You back away, mister," said Hutchers, in a threatening manner to the father. "Or I'll arrest you for obstruction of justice. You see if I don't."

Harry dropped his arms, in one futile sweep. The two cops pushed the older man aside, went to either side of the weeping younger man, and led him away. He sobbed loudly but did not resist.

Harry turned around, grabbed the back of his chair with both hands and leaned heavily against it.

"Thanks, Perce." Hutchers took his beat-up hat off, tipped it at her in a mock manner, and nodded. "I see you can be of some use."

"More than you, apparently," she said, as he moved to the door.

The detective replaced the hat on his head and laughed.

"Glad I amuse you, flatfoot." Percy followed him out and closed the door behind her. Reaching out, she grabbed Hutchers by the arm. He stopped and turned around to her, a questioning look on his face. Percy released his arm and put her finger to her lips in a shushing gesture, signaling for him to follow her down the hall and away from the office door.

Puzzled, he trailed behind, but not before he said, "Perce, I'm in a hurry."

"Listen, Hutchers," she said in a whisper, "you got the right man for slugging me, but I'm not so sure about the murders."

"What are you talking about? You handed him over to us on a silver platter. There's this journal where he admits it. Maybe I can get a day off now." He waved the book under her nose.

"I know, I know," she said, pushing the book away. "But I'm thinking."

"Ah, jeesh," he said out loud then lowered his voice with a glance around him. "It's no good when a woman starts thinking, particularly you."

"Oh, shut up. Hutchers, did you dust the handbag for prints?"

He stared at her. "Lily's bag? Yeah, sure we did. You think the DA would let us get away with not doing something like that?"

"Inside *and* out?"

"What do you mean, 'inside and out'? Why the hell would we dust the inside of a purse, Perce?"

Again with the double purse thing. The man's got a thing.

"You told me, yourself, the gun was wiped clean of prints. If she was smart enough to wipe the gun clean, why would she be stupid enough to put the weapon back in her own bag and stow it under the elf? I think it's a frame." Percy poked him on the chest with her index finger for emphasis. "Check the inside of the bag, Hutchers. You might come up with something that surprises you."

His eyes narrowed on her. "What do you know that I don't?"

"I'm just thinking it out, Hutchers. That's all I'm doing."

Hutchers wasn't satisfied. "Listen, Perce, I'm working on so many cases right now, I haven't had a day off in two months. I got better things to do...."

"Speaking of your cases, you find Danny DeLuca yet?"

"Funny you should ask. They thought they had him over in Jersey an hour ago, but it was a false alarm."

"Good to know."

"Now I'm your personal information center. I swear, Perce..." The detective broke off, slapped his battered fedora on his head, stepped around her, and marched down the hallway toward the exit.

"Hutchers," Percy called after him, her voice urgent and commanding.

He stopped abruptly and still with his back to her, let out a huge sigh. The detective wheeled around.

Percy glanced at Harry's office door then hurried up the detective. She didn't speak until they were almost nose to nose. "I'm telling you," she whispered. "Check the inside of the bag." She stressed each word as she spoke. "Please."

"Ah, nuts. All right, already, I'll do it." He shook a finger at her. "But if I don't find anything other than your little lady's prints, you owe me."

"I'll buy you a hotdog, Nathan's finest." She grinned. "Maybe two."

He gave her an annoyed look then relented and laughed, shaking his head.

"You're on," He said, pivoted, and continued down the hall. "But Jesus, am I a jackass or what," she heard him say to himself right before he hit the exit.

Percy paused outside of Harry's office door, not looking forward to the exchange that would probably follow.

A parent can be pretty fierce when it comes to protecting their kid. And forget about something like this. We're talking murder.

Expecting the worst, she opened the door. Harry, seated at his desk, didn't turn around when he heard the door close but his head popped up. He shook it, as if in disgust, while Percy walked to the edge of his desk. They both were silent for a moment.

"How could you let them do that?" Harry said after a beat, staring at the blank wall in front of him. His voice had a chiding but defeated air. "You know he didn't kill anybody."

"Tell me about Gertie."

"Gertie? You mean Gertrude, my bookkeeper?" Harry swiveled in his chair around to her, coming to life as he tried to digest the question. Percy could see his mind grappling with the change in subject. "What about her?"

"What was she doing here so late? Why did she have so much access to this building? The truth now. All games are over."

"She...Gertrude...We..."

"Used to have 'relations'? I believe that's what the word is for it now."

Harry bristled. "Listen, you don't know what it's like being married to Rita. She's --"

"Spare me the 'my wife doesn't understand me' routine," Percy interrupted. "I don't want to hear it; I don't care. I want to know about Gertie and her little trips in the tunnels."

"What makes you think she was in the tunnels?" His voice held a challenge, but he picked up a paper on his desk with shaky hands, pretending to read the contents.

"The first time I saw her, her costume was covered with schmutz, just like my clothes are now. It doesn't take much to figure out that's how it got so dirty."

"Where'd you learn a word like 'schmutz'?" He smiled up at her suddenly.

"You live in the tenements of New York, you learn a lot of words. But scratch the charm, Harry. I'm not one of your business pals or girlfriends, either. You've got three seconds to tell me the truth or I'm going to make you sorry for not being square with me. I'm running out of patience."

Harry ran a pudgy, red hand over his face before answering. Percy waited.

"You're right," he said, in a weary voice. "I told her not to wear that costume when she went down there, but would she listen to me? No. Gertrude was a strange one, but she spent a lot of time with Ernie. Companionship, you know; his pal. They'd wander around in the tunnels together for hours, just the two of them. I could never figure it out, myself, but she was great in the hay, you know?" He gave Percy a weak, self deprecating look and turned away. "Sometimes she'd bring back odd things from down there. Like once she brought back this crappy old doll --"

"Sometimes she'd bring back a piece of jewelry, too," Percy interjected. "Not quite so crappy."

Harry flushed and turned away. "I wouldn't know about that."

"Sure you would."

Anger and bile seem to come up from his gut. "Listen, nobody got hurt." He sputtered, as he threw the papers to his desk. "And it was only lately. Besides, that jeweler never said nothing and they were only little pieces, now and then. Not too much. Most times I'd take it away from her and make Ernie put it back before they noticed. Like I say…"

"She was great in the hay," Percy finished for him.

Harry grunted but didn't say anything.

"You're quite a piece of work, Harry, you know that? You shouldn't even own an animal."

"What?" The change in subject flummoxed him. He looked at her, his eyes searching hers for an answer. She didn't give any. Harry gave up and said, "This will kill his mother. Ernest didn't hurt anybody. He's just…different."

"Who wouldn't be, living down there like a sewer rat? Have you no shame?"

Harry turned on her. "You don't know anything. All his life everybody's thought the worst of him, treated him like a monster. He couldn't even go to school like a normal kid. I'm the one who found him those prescription tinted glasses so he could see. I'm the one that taught him to read, for Christ's sake. This is my reward for it." He cradled his head in his arms and fought back tears. "Even his own mother wanted to put him in a home but once I found out he liked being in the basement, I just couldn't do it. He's my only son." He looked up, wet eyes glistening. "You have children, Lady?"

"Yeah, I do."

"Then you understand," Harry said, pressing his advantage.

"Maybe I do. Maybe I don't." She took out her bag of pistachios and popped one in her mouth.

He shrugged his shoulders and picked up a pencil, tapping it on the hard surface of the desk. Both listened to the chaotic rhythm for a moment before Harry broke the silence, speaking almost to himself.

"This way I could see him every day. He was happy down there, happy. He had his tunnels and his books."

Percy dropped into the chair next to the desk and leaned back. It felt good to sit. Her head began to ache a little and she wished she had an aspirin. She ate another pistachio.

"But they're tearing down his tunnels and according to his journal, he was going to blow this place up rather than lose it. That's what he wrote, Harry."

"Oh phsaw," Harry said, dismissively. "How could he blow the place up? He doesn't have anything but a box of old firecrackers. Most of them too wet to light, anyway. He was just angry because...." Harry broke off. "He was just trying to pay me back."

"For selling the building out from under him?"

Harry nodded but looked away. His head jerked back to Percy. "How'd you know?"

"What are the chances anybody could swing a deal to rent this place for only two months out of the year, year after year, unless you owned it? Prime real estate being what it is."

Harry shrugged. "Okay, so I'm selling the place, but I didn't want anybody to know I own it. I was trying to shift things around first...."

"Trying to get out of paying some taxes, eh?"

"That's none of your business." Anger, almost fury, swept across his features.

"Don't be surprised at what I'm making my business." Percy's voice was calm and final.

Harry's anger vanished as it came, replaced by defeat. "Aw, do what you like, I can't stop you. I'm getting out, anyway, liquidating everything. We're moving down to Florida. I'm retiring, starting a new life. My wife's already down there."

"What about Ernie? What happens to him?"

"There's a place called Cypress Haven where we can all live together. He'll be taken care of." Harry threw the pencil down then leaned back, shriveling into himself. "Oh, God, I'm so tired. It's almost a relief to get all this out in the open."

"I bet it is." Percy looked at Harry with compassion for the first time.

He turned to her again. This time his eyes were clear but burning with sincerity. "He didn't kill anyone, I swear, lady. Look, I'm sorry he hit you. He panicked. He was trying to be like Dick Tracy, but when he realized what he did, he ran up here and begged for my help. By the time we got down there, you were gone. We couldn't find you. We looked everywhere. Then I thought, he'd made it all up. He does that now and then. He can't always tell what's real and what isn't. It was hard to convince him it was just his imagination but I almost did. Until you and the cops arrived," he added.

"And you found out it wasn't his imagination. He coshed me on the head and tied me up for real."

"I know." Harry closed his eyes and looked away, seemingly the weight of the world on his shoulders. "This will kill his mother. She's sensitive, delicate. Always has been ever since he was born. She's playing mahjong right now in Boca Raton with no idea, no idea at all. Boca Raton, you know what that means?"

"Yeah, mouth of the rat. It's Spanish."

Harry went on as if she hadn't answered. "She never liked him being here. I was the one that convinced her."

"You got to stop trying to convince people of things. It's causing a lot of trouble." Percy stood and looked down at him, studying him hard. "You're the other end of the *ratón*, as far as I'm concerned, Harry, but you've given me a few things to think about. One more thing, Ernie have a car?"

"A car? He can't drive a car. Hell, he fell off his tricycle so much when he was a kid, I had to take it away from him. Something about his peripheral vision."

"That's what I thought."

He looked up at her with pathetic eagerness. "Does that mean you'll help clear my son? I'll hire you. I'll make it worth your while. I can see you know what you're doing."

"Everybody wants to hire me lately. Must be something in the air." She cracked another pistachio and chewed on the nut before saying, "For the record, you can't hire me. Conflict of interest." She tossed the shells into the ashtray.

Crestfallen, Harry nodded in agreement but waved her away with a hand. Percy started for the door, turning back to him with an afterthought.

"Oh and by the way, Harry, don't look for the dog."

"The dog?" He spun his chair around to the woman, his face revealing total puzzlement. "My dog?"

"Not anymore."

She slammed the door behind her.

Chapter Twenty-three

Percy sat in the car parked at the curb of her building. The street was teaming with people going home, ending their work day. Everywhere she saw additional smiles and joviality, more happiness than usual. Mothers spoke with extra tolerance, and, wonder of wonder, children paid attention. They played on the sidewalk and in the sparsely trafficked street with added friendship with one another, too. Lovers, oblivious to everyone else, seemed more in love than usual, all due to the holiday season.

Percy, an eternal pragmatist, had always been partial to Christmas for this reason. While she acknowledged the baser part of human nature, she was secretly delighted when people behaved better than expected. Christmas seemed to bring that out in humanity. And the look on her own son's face each Christmas morning clinched it for her.

Every now and then the dog moved closer to her from his side of the car seat, nuzzling her with his nose. Percy reached out an automatic hand and stroked his tufted forehead, never losing the thoughts she'd been arranging in her mind.

Okay, Percy, none of this feels right. It's all too easy. Yeah, the Ernie kid conked you on the head but that doesn't mean he's a

murderer. Of course, it doesn't mean he isn't either. But I got this gut feeling, he ain't the one, no matter what he wrote in his journal.

Now his father I could see. Harry is one selfish SOB. He knew about the tunnels and he was schtupping the Christmas angel, too. Maybe…

She sat for a moment letting Harry's possible guilt seep into her, took a deep breath, and shook her head. The detective looked out the windshield at the busy street filled with children and adults going about their normal, daily lives, except for one.

A lone man, several car lengths down, stood on the sidewalk and leaned against a streetlamp, an open newspaper covering his face. Fidgeting fingers and flexing arm muscles told her that behind this paper was a very wound-up guy. Without seeing his face, she could tell he was young, hardly out of his teens, but with a wariness that comes when you know the world is against you and has been for some time.

Feeling a chill, she turned on the car's heater, which mercifully still worked. The dog climbed in her lap, jamming himself between her and the steering wheel, and licked her face.

"You need to go for a walk, doggy?" She stroked a long, soft ear.

She glanced at the man again then at her watch, moving her wrist to catch the light from her own streetlight overhead. "We've been sitting here for nearly an hour." She glanced up at the windows of her apartment on the fourth floor. "Time to go and get some more answers, doggy. But first a walk to empty out your bladder."

Still thinking, she turned off the motor, stepped out of the car, and removed the leather belt from her slacks. "It's a good thing I'm fat, doggy. My belt makes for a nice, long leash." She looped the belt around his collar. "Come on, let's go take care of your business and then mine."

The dog hopped out and began to circle, searching for a spot. Meanwhile, Percy looked around her and noticed the approach of a police officer making his rounds. Chewing gum and walking down the street swinging his baton, Jimmy O'Leary, younger brother of Tom, waved when he saw her. Red hair similar in color to hers, he had often been mistaken for her kid brother when they were growing up. Along with his Irish family, he moved into the neighborhood years ago and still lived in the same apartment with his parents.

"Hey, fuzz, they let you coppers chew gum on the job?" She yelled loud enough that several people nearby, knowing both parties, began to laugh.

"Hey, gumshoe," Jimmy hollered back. "They still leaving you loose on the street? There's no telling what lowlife you're going to run into around here."

They both laughed and embraced briefly, he a good four inches shorter than she.

"How you doing, Percy? You and the family doing okay?" His grin practically broke his face, as did hers. They rarely met, but when they did, their decades-old friendship came shining through.

"We're good, I'm good, Jimmy."

"Haven't seen you for a while, but Tom tells me he caught you uptown at a fancy jewelry store. Says you're working on a case about a dead elf."

"Yeah, a not so fancy murder. You know how that goes, Jimmy."

"I do. Looking for a little action, myself." He leaned in. "I'm kind of tired of walking the beat. Like to get myself a fancy desk job, a promotion, you know?"

"Well, then this may just be your lucky day, Jimmy O'Leary." She leaned back at him and whispered in his ear. "I think I got a pretty big collar for you."

Jimmy pulled back and gave her a puzzled, surprised look, but said no more and waited.

Percy patted him on the shoulder, while continuing to speak in a low voice. "See that guy back there reading the paper and leaning against the lamppost?"

He nodded imperceptibly, his hazel eyes bright and alert. He was a good cop.

"Unless I'm wrong – and I seldom am –"

"Sez you," he interjected with a wink, but his demeanor didn't shift from prepared for action. "So who is he?"

"Don't look now, but that man is the escaped felon, Danny DeLuca."

"Are you kidding me?" His interruption was more of an explosion.

"Shhhh! Keep your voice down. You know me, I never kid a kidder. So here's my idea. Let's you and me saunter over there easy-like. You grab him, I'll help you, and then you make sergeant. Sort of my Christmas present to you. How does that sound?"

Jimmy hesitated. "You sure about this?"

"Yeah, look for yourself. He fits the description and the kicker is he's got a tattoo on his left wrist that says 'Mother knows best', just like the guy in all these wanted posters."

"What's he doing here?"

"Looking for his mother? Checking out real estate? How the hell should I know? Now are you making the collar and getting yourself promoted or am I making a citizen's arrest?"

Jimmy puffed up his chest and put his right hand on his revolver. "Let's go."

Side by side, man, woman, and dog slowly walked in the direction of the reading man. Percy closed in on the man's right, Jimmy stayed to the left.

"Mind telling me what you're doing in our neighborhood, mister?" Jimmy's voice lost the easy-going, friendly tone he'd used with Percy and gained an authoritative toughness.

The man didn't respond at first then slowly lowered the newspaper. He gave a quick glance at the uniformed officer of the law and made a move to flee. Percy stuck her

booted right foot out in front of him. Danny DeLuca tripped and fell to the ground. Jimmy was on him but the scuffle was brief. The cop was not only the larger man but faster and more practiced at his craft.

Percy stood back, as did the dog and the rest of the neighborhood, and watched the law vs. the criminal scene unfolding between them.

"You okay down there, Jimmy?" She leaned over the policeman lying on the back of the struggling man who was face down on the sidewalk.

"You want to hand me my cuffs, Percy? They're in my back pocket."

"Sure." Percy reached down pulled the handcuffs out and dangled them in front of her friend's hand.

"Thanks." Jimmy cuffed the man's wrists with expertise and hauled DeLuca up with him as he stood. He held the man by the scruff of the neck. "You answer me now. You Danny DeLuca?"

When the man didn't reply, Jimmy slammed the man's face against the steel frame of the lamppost, eliciting a groan from the cuffed man and a bark from the dog.

"Yes, yes, I'm Danny Deluca. Don't hurt me anymore."

"Easy, Jimmy." Percy made a face. "Don't get blood all over the lamppost. How do you think that's going to make the neighborhood look to passersby?"

"Shut up, Percy."

"And you're welcome, Jimmy."

"Oh, yeah, thanks." He turned briefly in Percy's direction with a nod of his head then gave his attention back to his collar. "Come on, you. We're taking a short walk to the station."

Percy reached out a hand. "Before you go, let me ask this lug a question, okay?"

"Go ahead, but make it quick."

An angry red welt was forming above DeLuca's right eye, easily seen under the light.

"How'd you know to come here?" Percy stared into his face.

When he didn't answer, Jimmy shook him and said in a threatening tone, "Answer the lady."

"A phone call. I got a phone call."

"When?"

"At the jail a couple of days ago."

"Who was it?"

"They didn't say. Some man. He told me about you, gave me your address, and said to follow you. Said you'd know where she was."

"You mean Lily?"

"I ain't talking no more."

"Who's Lily?" Jimmy turned a cop's face toward Percy.

"My maid." Percy's answer was terse.

"Yeah, yeah, a likely story." Jimmy grabbed DeLuca's shoulder, held tight, and pulled him in the direction of the police station down the block. "Let's go, pal, and you do anything funny, I'll shoot to kill and make captain."

Danny DeLuca, head down, stumbled alongside the policeman to the station at the end of the block.

* * * *

"Hello, everybody," Percy yelled from the front door. "Anybody here? I've got a surprise," she sang out.

Her bedroom door flung open, banging against the wall. "Mommy," said Oliver, "You're home!" The joy on his face from seeing his mother was quickly transferred to the dog.

"A dog! You brought a dog!" The boy ran and slid forward on his knees, embracing the canine. The dog, in turn, began to wag his tail furiously, licking the boy's face everywhere. The kitchen door swung open, and Lily came out, wearing an apron and carried an eggbeater with her. Surprise and delight covered her face, when she saw boy and dog.

"Mommy," Oliver giggled in between licks of the dog. "Where did he come from? Can we keep him? What's his name? Gosh, he's so cute."

The dog ran in circles around the boy, yipping and coming back for more licks.

"Well, this seems to be a marriage made in heaven," Percy observed. She kneeled down and faced her son, the dog scooting in the middle, bouncing up and down, tongue lagging out at the side of his mouth.

"He's from Santa Claus, sweetie, and he might be your early Christmas present."

"He is?" The boy wrapped arms around the dog and cuddled him. "Just what I asked for! My own dog."

"Not so fast. Oliver, a dog is not a toy. He's a living being. With him comes a lot of responsibility."

Her voice had taken on a serious, lecturing tone, and Oliver stopped wiggling and gave his mother his undivided attention. Even the dog sobered, sat still, and stared at Percy. Two sets of eyes stared up in rapt attention. She fought the smile coming to her face.

"He needs to be walked at least twice a day, rain or shine, whether you feel like it or not. He needs to be fed twice a day, too, with plenty of fresh water always available. He's in your care now. He needs you to take care of him, understand, son?"

The boy nodded with a gravity that almost made Percy laugh. She kept the soberness to her voice. "Do you promise to do your best? Do you promise to take care of this little doggy?"

Oliver nodded again, his chin hit the front button of his shirt with every descent of his head.

"Okay, then. You can keep him."

"Yah!" said Oliver. The dog yipped and crawled into Oliver's lap. Oliver hugged him and the dog closed his eyes in contentment. "What's his name, Mommy?"

"He doesn't have one that I know of."

"Do I get to name him?" His mother nodded. "Fred! I'm going to call him Fred."

Percy glanced at Lily, acknowledging her for the first time. The both said in unison,

"Fred?"

"That's my best friend's name at school. Fred. I like the name Fred," said the boy, standing.

Percy moved to Lily's side. Both women stood watching the boy and dog.

"You realize," Percy whispered to Lily, "In about two days he'll forget and I'll be doing all of that myself. But it's good for Oliver to try his hand at responsibility."

'You're a good mother, Miss Cole," said Lily.

"When I'm around. Speaking of being around, where is everybody?"

"Your father got a call from the doctor a few hours ago. A bed opened earlier than expected."

"So he's at the hospital?"

"Yes. Your brother dropped by and picked him up. He's nice, your brother."

"Jude is. Where's my mother? With them?"

"Yes. She's going to spend the night at the hospital."

"And Sera, where's she?"

"She had a date."

"Aw, that girl," Percy commented in disapproval.

"She wanted to go with them, but your father wouldn't hear of it. He wanted her to go on with her plans, he said."

Percy didn't reply. Grim lips formed a thin line on her face. She gestured with her head toward the kitchen, pushed the door open, and went inside, followed by Lily.

"How was Pop doing?"

"Okay. Not too bad. He looked like he was in a certain amount of pain."

"I know. We're hoping this new Penicillin drug will help."

Lily looked down at her feet, hesitating before she spoke. "If you need any money…" Her voice tapered off.

"Thank you, Lily, but no." Percy patted her lightly on the shoulder. "And thanks for babysitting Oliver for me. Let's sit down for a moment." Percy pulled back a kitchen chair, gestured to it, and sat down at the table across from it.

A deep sigh escaped from Lily. "Another question and answer period?"

"More like true confessions."

Lily sat down and looked earnestly into Percy's face, much the way Oliver had moments before.

"First, I want to relieve your mind about something. Danny DeLuca has been caught and is on his way back to jail."

Tension seemed to sweep away from the girl. She threw her head back and closed her eyes. "Thank God. I was so scared, not just for me but for you and your family."

"That's one problem out of the way, but to move along to a few more, let me say first, I think you trust me, Lily. You may not like me, but you trust me."

"You're wrong, Miss Cole. I do like you. I'm a little afraid of you, but I like you." Lily opened her eyes and smiled tentatively. Her face was devoid of makeup and her wavy, dark hair was pulled back off her face. Large brown eyes looked up at Percy with the same air of trust and wonderment she'd just seen in her son and the dog.

Jeesh, she's hardly more than a kid. She could practically be my daughter, for cripes sake. Oh great. I really am an old broad.

"Well, thank you, Lily, I think," she said. "I know in some instances, I've been hard on you."

"You were just doing your job, Miss Cole."

"Yeah, that I was and am. It's nothing personal." Both women smiled at each other, a tenuous friendship beginning. "How are you feeling, Lily? Still got that upset stomach?"

"Not too much," she replied. "It's mostly in the morning, anyway. By the evening I'm fine."

"How's the ache in the small of your back? And your breasts, are they swollen or sore?"

"Now that you mention it, I --" Lily froze midsentence, with her hand half-way to the small of her back. Her face took on a look of surprise then comprehension. Her eyes focused not on her surroundings, but somewhere within herself.

"That's what I think, too," Percy said. "But you'd better go to a doctor to make sure."

The kitchen door burst open and Oliver ran in followed by the newly named Fred. A laughing child was chased by a barking dog in a game clearly a timeless favorite of all small children and dogs. Oliver ran in circles around the two women at the table, the dog happily behind. Percy grabbed her son by the arm on one of his runs.

"Oliver, stop." The boy came to a stop and looked expectantly at his mother. Her voice was gentle but firm. "You can't play with the dog inside the house the same way you play with him outside, understand?"

"Yes, Mommy."

"Being tomorrow is Saturday and there's no school, go put on your coat and hat. You can take Fred down to the courtyard behind the building. But you are to stay right under the kitchen window and near the lamppost where I can see you at all times, okay?"

"Yes, ma'am."

"And only for fifteen minutes. Then come back upstairs, you have to go to bed. Did you do your homework?"

"Yes, ma'am."

The boy headed back to the kitchen door, followed by the dog still dragging the makeshift leash.

"And Oliver, hold onto the belt I put on his collar on your way down the stairs. We'll buy him a proper leash tomorrow but meanwhile, we don't want him to run away."

A look of horror crossed Oliver's face. "No, ma'am."

He spoke with such earnestness, his face wearing such a sincere look, Percy had to bite her lip to hide the smile. She fought the urge to cover him with kisses and responded to his solemnity with only a nod.

"All right then. You go downstairs and have a good time with Fred."

The boy went out, trailed by the dog, and the door swung to a close. A moment passed with Percy watching the silent, closed door. Then she turned back to Lily, who hadn't moved, probably still lost in her own thoughts.

"I love it when he calls me ma'am. I'm enjoying it while I can. He'll probably stop soon enough." She studied the girl for a few moments, pushed the chair back, and got up slowly. "I should take an aspirin. Maybe some food will help my headache. Got anything to eat around here?"

Lily's mind seemed to come back into focus. She rose and crossed to the stove, standing in front of the oven. "I kept a plate of meatloaf warm for you in the oven. I make mine with shaved carrots. It adds a sweetness--" She broke off abruptly, covered her face with her hands and sobbed into them. "Oh, my God. I can't be pregnant. I can't be."

Percy came up behind Lily, turned her around, and gave her small, shaking body a quick, motherly embrace. "Listen, you'll go to a doctor and you'll see. If so, it's not like you're going to starve to death. You've got the money to have

a kid. Actually about two dozen kids, if you want. You're not alone in this, unless you want to be."

"It's not always about money," Lily said, her voice quivering with bitterness.

"No, but it often is. If you really don't want a kid, there are always backstreet doctors--"

"I'd never do that," Lily interrupted Percy with a burst of anger.

Percy put her hands up in surrender and backed away. "Then there you go," she said in an easy tone. "You've already made one decision. The others will come as you go along."

Lily cooled as quickly as she'd flared. "I'm sorry and you're right. Besides, maybe I could have someone as wonderful as Oliver in my life. That wouldn't be so bad." She forced a smile, grabbed the corners of her apron with both hands to use as oven mitts, bent over, and took the plate out of the oven. "I made potatoes au gratin, too. They're my favorite." The two women smiled at one another.

Percy lost her smile and watched Lily spoon out potatoes onto the plate. Percy crossed over to the kitchen window, raised it up, and leaned out, looking down to make sure her child was there. "Oliver," she called. "Stay close to the light where I can see you at all times, okay? Don't play over in the shadows."

"Okay, Mommy," he shouted up. "I brought my ball down with me. Can I throw it to Fred?"

"If you throw it easy and not out of the yard. And don't make too much noise. Remember, it's getting late and some people are going to bed soon."

"Okay, Mommy!" The dog let out two short barks, sounding like he too, would not make unnecessary noise.

Percy turned and looked at Lily, now fussing with the plate of warm food in her hand. Lily's body, though, had a tense edge to it, as if all the muscles were waiting for something to happen. Her eyes darted around the room,
maybe looking for a peaceful place to land. Percy felt sorrier for her than she had for anyone in a long time.

"Have you ever heard a boy's voice so delirious with happiness?" She smiled at Lily. "Even the dog sounds happy."

Lily brightened for a moment, picked up a fork and napkin and scurried over to Percy, offering the food and tableware. "You're probably going to want to sit here and watch Oliver out the window."

"You're probably right." Percy grabbed the back of a chair and pulled it over. She lowered the window but sat watching her son. She spread the napkin in her lap and took the plate and fork. "I'm sure this looks nuts to you, but--"

Lily smiled. "No, I understand. You want to make sure he's safe."

"Yeah, something like that."

"Parents want their children to be safe...usually." It was a sad statement, as if Lily knew times when parents didn't care if their children are safe or not. Head down, she went to the sink and began to wash dishes. Her face had a maturity about it, so different from the short time ago, when she seemed to have the face of a child.

Percy cut off a large piece of meatloaf with her fork, holding the plate in the other hand. She crammed it into her mouth and chewed with her eyes closed in appreciation. After swallowing, she said, "God, girl, you've got to open your own restaurant. The world needs this food."

Lily laughed lightly. "Thanks. Maybe I'll do that one of these days."

Percy took another bite, listening to the sounds of her son and the dog below, but all the while looking at Lily. "Lily, you're going to have to talk to me. I know there's something bad between you and your father and I want to know what it is."

"I..." The girl hesitated. She shook her head and dried a cup with gusto, concentrating on it.

"Pay attention to me, Lily." The girl put down the cup and stared at Percy. "I wouldn't be asking if it wasn't important, even crucial. We're at the eleventh hour. I need to

know. What happened in the past? What's going on between you and your father?"

The girl dried her hands and went over to the table. She sat in one of the chair and looked straight ahead. She nodded to no one in particular, maybe to all the ghosts in the past.

"All right, I'll tell you. I've never told anyone what happened that day."

"What day?"

"The day my mother died." She took a deep breath, held it and released it with a hissing sound. "I was seven years old. It actually started the night before. My mother and father had a terrible, terrible fight. I've never heard so much yelling."

"What was the fight about?"

"At the time, I didn't understand what was going on, but now…" She turned and looked at Percy for the first time. "I was only seven. But as the years went by and I grew up, I began to understand what happened that night…and the following day." Lily looked away again. She picked up the corner of the tablecloth and fussed with it absentmindedly before she went on.

"My father found out my mother was cheating on him and confronted her. Apparently she'd been doing it for some time when he'd be away on his buying trips. And not just with one man, but several." Lily let out a choked sob. "This is hard, hard to say, even after all these years. My mother had been drinking. She did that a lot. That night she said terrible things to father, nasty cruel things. Things like him not being man enough for her. He called her a tramp or a whore. "

I can't remember which one; I was so terrified. I'd never known him to raise his voice to her before. I... I think she slapped him. I don't know for sure everything that went on inside that room but you could feel the hate coming out at you, even through the closed door. At first, I was outside her room in the hallway," Lily explained, glancing over at Percy. "They had separate bedrooms by this time. I heard a vase or something, smashing against a wall then a piece of furniture being overturned. That's when I ran and hid under my bed. I must have been there, sobbing for hours. I don't know what happened between them after that. I was too frightened to stay." Lily reached out both hands and smoothed the tablecloth before going on.

"Father came into my room several hours later and found me asleep under the bed. He pulled me out and put me to bed. He kept telling me not to be afraid; it would be all right. My mother never came to me that night." Lily stopped speaking, brushed at wet eyes, and was silent.

"Go on," Percy demanded.

"The next morning I woke up late, went downstairs, had some breakfast then went to mother's room. I knocked on the door and when she didn't answer, I didn't think anything of it. She often slept late and didn't answer. I would usually go away for an hour or two, but that morning, I didn't go away. I pushed the door open and went inside. My mother had been sick for weeks with something called 'walking pneumonia' but you could never get her to stay home. She was out every night, dancing and partying, no matter what the doctor said. Gosh, she was so beautiful, my mother," Lily said with a faint smile.

"I'll bet she was."

"Anyway, the first thing I noticed when I snuck into her room was it was freezing. The window was wide open, even thought we'd had a freak snowstorm and it had been snowing all night. Mother was lying on the bed in a sheer nightgown, completely uncovered, still, so still. Even at that age, I knew something was wrong. I called out to her but she didn't answer. I closed the window and scraped the snow off the sill and floor, running back and forth, throwing it into the sink, trying to clean up. Then I covered her up as best I could."

"You didn't think to call your father?"

Lily shook her head. "I knew they were mad at each other. I wanted to make her better, first. Maybe I wanted to be the one to make everything better, I don't know. I kept shaking her, trying to get her to wake up. Sometimes when she'd been drinking, it would take several minutes to wake her up. When I touched her face, it was burning hot. Just as I was about to panic, father came into the room. When he saw her, he pulled me away. He was rough about it. I'd never known him to be rough with me before. He called the doctor and the doctor came right away. They took my mother to the hospital but she never regained consciousness and died a day later."

Lily began to sob. "He killed her." Lily turned a wet face to Percy. "He opened the window that night and stripped off the covers. He hated her that night. I could hear it in his voice. He knew she'd been sick. That night she was drunker than usual. She wouldn't know anything he did to her. But her body did and she died."

"Did you ever confront your father? Talk to him about this?" Lily shook her head slowly. "Jesus, what is the matter with you people?"

"I didn't realize most of this until years later, maybe when I was twelve or thirteen. At the time, I was scared. None of it made sense."

"But later?"

"I would think about that night and the next morning over and over again, time after time. The older I got, the more I understood what was really going on, what happened. But by then, it was too late. I tried to hate him, but I couldn't. She was so awful, I see that. I still don't hate him. I know he had is reasons, but he killed my mother. I know he was angry and hurt but...."

Percy stood, went to the table and set down her empty plate. She returned to the window and raised it.

"Oliver," she called down. Her son stopped bouncing the ball and looked up. "Come on upstairs now. Time for bed." She lowered the window and turned to Lily, who was staring down at the table, but not really seeing it. "Thanks for telling me. I can see you've been living a hell on earth and not much of it was your own making."

"But I've still made a lot of my own mistakes."

"But you've still made a lot of your own mistakes," Percy agreed.

"Maybe this baby is my chance to make a fresh start."

"Listen, if you got troubles a lot of times a kid can only make them worse. Having a baby isn't the magic cure-all but

for what it's worth, I wouldn't trade Oliver for anything. He's my life."

Lily looked at Percy with searching eyes. "What are you going to do? Now that you know the truth about my father and mother?"

"First, I'm going to put my son to bed and then I'm going out again. I need to take care of something. You okay with watching Oliver while I'm gone?"

"Of, course."

"That was fast. I think I hear him at the door."

Trailed by Lily, Percy went to the kitchen door, opened it and looked down the hall.

The front door flew open and Sera came in. "Hi, everybody," she said when she saw Percy and Lily standing at the end of the hall in the kitchen doorway. Hi, you two."

"What are you doing home?" Percy questioned. She stepped into the hall. Lily followed, both women letting the kitchen door close behind them.

"I thought you were out on a date," Lily said.

"Oh, that." Sera's tone was noncommittal. "I wasn't in the mood. Besides, he got fresh so I ditched him and came home by bus."

"Leave the door open," Percy ordered as her sister started to close it. "Oliver is coming up from the courtyard with his new dog."

"Dog?" Sera let go of the door and moved down the hall toward Percy and Lily.

The door swung wide open. Instead of Oliver, Detective Hutchers stepped inside, and paused with a knowing stance in the doorway.

"I thought so." Hutchers looked directly at Lily then Percy.

"What are you doing here, Hutchers? You have no right busting in here--" Percy stepped in front of Lily. Hutchers and Percy moved closer to each other, facing off.

"And you have no right shielding a person wanted for murder. I came here right after they booked that freak. I had a sneaking feeling you were hiding something....or someone."

"Come on, you know Lily didn't do it, Hutchers. Use your brain." Percy challenge was said with exasperation.

"You're the one who convinced me the guy in the tunnel couldn't have done it. So we're back to her." He looked over Percy's shoulder and pointed at Lily standing in front of the kitchen door, not moving.

The sound of Oliver's footsteps thudding down the building's hallway stopped Percy's reply. She hurried toward the front door. Boy and dog raced inside and scooted around her, only stopping when coming toe to toe with Hutchers.

Confused, Oliver looked around him, but knew something was happening. The dog came closer to Oliver and sat at his feet. Both looked up at the statue-still man.

"Oliver," said Percy. "Take Fred into the bedroom and put your pajamas on. I'll be right in."

Oliver picked up the leash, looked up at the burly man standing beside him, and went into Percy's bedroom leading the dog without saying a word.

"What's going on around here, anyway?" asked Sera. "Every time I walk in this door, something's going on around here."

"Sera, go help Oliver into his pajamas and keep the dog off the bed, would you?" Percy said.

"Sure, sure. Trying to get me out of the way, but I don't take offense." Sera scurried into Percy's bedroom, shutting the door behind her.

"Hutchers, Lily in innocent --" Percy began.

Hutchers shook a finger in Percy's face and interrupted her. "You need to shut up. I should run you in right now for aiding and abetting a criminal. But I'm not going to unless you give me trouble. I'm going to say I apprehended this Waller dame as she was approaching your apartment."

He turned to Lily. "You get your coat; you're coming with me." His attention went back to Percy. "You, don't press your luck." He looked over Percy's shoulder at the small brunette, who hadn't moved an inch. "Get your hat and coat, Miss Waller, like I said. You're under arrest."

"Listen, Hutchers, Lily didn't kill the elf. I've almost got the proof. Give me another twenty-four hours, please, and I'll give you your real killer."

"You've got a lot of nerve, Perce. You keep talking, I'm going to run you in, too. Let's go, Waller. Right now before I get mad."

Percy stepped nose to nose with him, as Lily made a move to the coat rack. "Sometimes you can be so stupid, Hutchers. I know you're sore at me and I suppose you've got every right to be, but--"

Lily laid a hand on Percy's arm. "It's all right, Miss Cole. I'm willing to go." She turned a pleading face to Hutchers. "I just hope I'm not in there too long."

Percy blocked her way for the moment. "I'll have you out before morning, I promise. But right now I'm going to have to do something you're not going to like, Lily. I want to

say I'm sorry about it upfront and get it out of the way." She stared down at the girl.

Lily gulped then nodded, but said nothing. As she turned around to remove her apron and don her coat, Percy turned on the detective saying in a low voice,

"Hutchers, she's pregnant. Don't take your anger at me out on her. Don't scare her or be any nastier than you have to be. You don't want her losing her baby."

Hutchers eyes opened wide at the pronouncement, but he didn't say a word. After a second, he nodded in agreement. He turned to Lily and his voice was gentler.

"Okay, Miss," he said touching her arm, "Come with me, please."

Lily turned to Percy, barely able to mask her fear.

"You'll be out by morning, Lily, I promise." Percy felt the need for reiteration. "Just hang on until then."

Lily tried to smile and managed a nod of her head. Percy watched them leave then shut the door.

And there goes five thousand smackers, too. Crap.

Chapter Twenty-four

Percy shut the motor off and starred at number Sixty-five Beekman Place. A three-story, red brick townhouse, it looked polished and elegant with its gleaming white trim. Window boxes and planters filled with hardier winter flowers, ivy, and evergreens lined the walkway and front porch. Even in the catches of winter, the streetlights showed a residence long on grooming and care, unlike most of the places Percy frequented.

Her hand reached inside the glove compartment and drew out the World War One pistol, a German Lugar semi-automatic. Percy's uncle had brought it back as a souvenir from the Great War, leaving it to her in his will. Well-oiled, she'd maintained it as impeccably as the landscaping she saw before her. Percy got out of the car and headed for the white, brass-trimmed door on the house. She reached inside her jacket, tucking the gun into the belt of her pants, a belt she'd taken back from her son and dog.

The polished and ornate brass handle gleamed in the light cast from the two frosted lights hanging on the wall on either side of the door. She fisted the knocker and banged it three times, hearing the sound resonate from inside. While Percy waited for the door to open, she read her wristwatch. Nine-thirty. Too late to call at someone's home, Emily Post would say.

But Emily Post isn't looking for a killer. All bets are off when you're looking for a murderer.

The door open slightly and a graying man of about sixty-five, impeccably dressed in a black suit, peered through the crack. He had an imperious look on his face. "Yes? May I help you?"

"You must be Hanson. Your bosses around?"

The man studied the woman, a look of distain crossing his face. His expression turned to puzzlement, but he did not open the door any wider. "I'm afraid the Wallers are dining and cannot be disturbed."

"That would be Waller senior and Waller junior, right?" Before the butler could answer, Percy pushed at the front door with both hands. Hanson lost his balance and took a step or two backward. Percy stepped inside.

"Now see here," Hanson said severely. "You cannot push your way in. Just who do you think you are?"

"I know who I am buster. Do you?" Percy moved around him and into the foyer. A quick glance around caused her to say, "Nice digs. The dining room this way?" She took large strides down the hallway toward a well-lit room.

Trying to keep up, Hanson sputtered. "See here, madam, you cannot disturb them --" Hanson interrupted himself as they both entered the dining room, he coming to a short stop at the threshold.

"Good evening, gentlemen," Percy said in a loud voice.

Both father and son sat opposite one another at one end of a mammoth dining room table, dark wood gleaming under the light of a crystal chandelier. In front of each man sat an elaborate set of plate ware and dining utensils. Silver and crystal goblets sparkled on two individual brocade placemats. Otherwise, the immense table was bare. The two men turned to her in surprise.

"So this is how the other half lives. I'll bet you still need some Pepto Bismol now and then."

The younger Waller was the first to recover and half rose from the table. "Miss Cole. I don't understand. Do you have news of Lily?" The older Waller remained seated, eyes narrowed, mouth grim.

"Forgive the intrusion, boys, but this won't take long. I --"

Hanson interrupted her with a snarl. "Should I call the police, Mr. Waller?" His question was directed at the senior Waller, who had yet to move. "I apologize, sir. I couldn't keep her out."

"Good idea! Let's call the cops. Allow me," Percy said, heading for the white French style phone resting on the end of a credenza. She picked up the phone and dialed zero.

"Miss Cole," said William Waller, now standing in front of his chair. "What is the meaning -"

"Shhh!" Percy put her finger to her lips then turned back to the phone but kept her eyes on the three men at the dining table. The other end answered.

"Hey, Matt. Persephone Cole here. How you doing? Uh-huh. Listen, is Hutchers there? Good. Tell him to get his duff and two of his finest over to Sixty-five Beekman Place right away. He has? Why has he been trying to reach me? I see. Well, he can talk to me when he gets here."

She hung up the phone and turned back to the three staring men. "Before we get to anything else, gentlemen," Percy said in a commanding voice, "I should tell you that Detective Hutchers arrested Lily for murdering Conrad Barnes about an hour ago. That's one of the reasons I'm here."

"Oh, my God," William Waller said, falling back into his chair. He threw a white linen napkin on the table with determination. "We've got to save her. I can't let her --" He stood again.

"Sit down, sit down. All in good time," Percy ordered. "We need to have a talk first and we don't have a lot of time." She turned around and faced the butler standing behind her.

"That means you, too, bub. Why don't you go join your employers at the other end of the table?" She circled behind him. "Oh, that's right. It's just one employer. Singular. You work for the senior Waller only, don't you? That leaves junior hanging out to dry most of the time, doesn't it?"

The elder man, who had remained silent and motionless, finally spoke. His gaze never left Percy standing at the other end of the table. "Hanson, call the police back. Tell them I want to file charges against this woman for breaking and entering."

Hanson made a move for the telephone. Percy reached inside her jacket and withdrew the pistol, brandishing it for all three men to see. Three startled men stared at her in horror.

"Sorry, gentlemen, but we're going to have to sit tight for awhile and I want you three where I can see you at all times. The cops will be here in about ten minutes, anyway. You can tell them anything you want to then." She turned back to Hanson, gesturing with the gun,

"Meanwhile, get back over there with those two, like I said."

The butler's face drained of color and he stumbled toward his master. He stood behind the senior Waller's chair, gaping at Percy.

"Miss Cole, have you lost your mind?" William Waller stuttered, nonetheless sitting back down.

The elder man was quiet and unmoved by having a gun waved in his direction. Percy directed her stare at him.

"If I have, Bill, it wouldn't be the first time," she answered then turned to his father. "For the record, Mr. Waller, I can't be arrested for breaking and entering. Your good man let me in, albeit a little reluctantly. Now I could get arrested for threatening you with a lethal weapon, but we're going to see how our little conversation goes before we get to that and just who gets arrested for what."

"What conversation?" William Waller looked from Percy to his father.

"I'm going to tell you both a story. Actually, I'm going to tell all three of you a story, because this involves you, too, Hanson. You see, this didn't start the night the elf was killed."

"What didn't start?" William Waller spoke up again.

"Now, shush, Bill. Let me tell it my way and don't interrupt me. I'll get to it," Percy ordered. "Does anybody call you Bill, I wonder? If not, they should. Might loosen you up a bit. Anyway, ten years ago your wife died, or should I say, your wife was murdered --" She left the rest of the sentence dangling.

"Murdered?" The son echoed the last word and it exploded in the still air.

"Yes, murdered, Bill. She was murdered in your house on Long Island. All this time, Lily thought you had done it."

"Me?" His voice came out more like a squeak than a sound.

"Before you came in and found Lily with her mother, your daughter had cleaned the snow off the floor and window sill, closed the window, and covered her back up with a blanket."

"Snow? What snow? I don't under --"

"If you don't let me finish, Bill, we're going to be here all night." Percy's voice had an impatient air. "Let's just say, all these years Lily thought it was you who opened the window and threw back the blankets on her drunken and sick mother that night, causing her to die the next day. When all the time, it was you," she said, pivoting. Percy focused the nozzle of the gun on the elder Waller. Waller senior remained implacable, but Hanson gasped, and took a guilty step back.

"Well, I see Hanson knew about this, too," Percy remarked. "As I'm sure he's known about everything else. The trusted, helping hand. Ah, they don't make dedicated servants like him, anymore."

"What are you talking about?" William Waller's voice was loud and firm. "Explain yourself, Miss Cole. My wife died of pneumonia, too much alcohol, and not taking care of herself."

"Let's just say she had a little help. Actually, a lot of help." Percy turned to his father. "Didn't she, sir?"

"You can't prove a thing," Waller senior stated. He wore a faint smile, but his eyes were cold.

"Father! Father, why aren't you denying these charges? I --
" Young Waller broke off, staring at his father.

"Be quiet, William. Hanson, do something." Waller senior waved a hand in the butler's direction.

Percy let out a small laugh. "Boy, you two are ones for the book. The feudal system is alive and well around here," Percy said, shaking her head.

Hanson made a move toward her. She leveled the pistol at him.

"Piece of advice, Hanson. Don't come at me if you like all your body parts the way they are. I mean, I know you'd do just about anything – and have – for your boss, but I don't think it involves getting shot."

Hanson swallowed hard and retreated back behind the elder Hanson's chair. Percy went on. "Besides, I'm not through talking yet and a good servant never interrupts. It's rude." She turned back to Lily's father. "To continue, your wife's murder, Bill, was only the first."

"That's ridiculous," William Waller contradicted, his voice hesitant but skeptical. "I know Father didn't like her, but why should he want my wife dead?"

Father and son looked at one another, as if there was no one else in the room. The elder man slammed his hand down on the table, rattling silver and crystal in a crescendo. He leaned across the table. The son drew back instinctively.

"William, you are so wanting, so inept. After all these years you have to ask why?" His voice was harsh and each word seemed to feed on the previous in hatred and contempt. "Why? You ask why? She was a harlot, a slut! Her wickedness made a mockery of our good name. I overheard the things she said to you. I listened to you whining, trying to reason with her. She passed out, you left her room, and I saw the opportunity. I took it, unlike you, you sniveling excuse for a man. I'm ashamed of you."

William stared slack-jawed at his father for a moment before saying, "But, Father, I was planning on divorcing her. I told her so that night."

The old man leaned in to stare his son down. "Do you think I was going to let you drag our family name through the newspapers with a divorce? The rumor mills were already alive with her despicable behavior. And you were so weak. You are so weak. She probably would have talked you into forgiving her, that sinful, tawdry woman. I was trying to salvage what remained of our reputation."

"I can't believe it," William said slowly. "I simply can't believe it. You killed Helen?" William gaped at his father.

"I did not kill her. She killed herself." Senior Waller's reply was infuriated in tone, as if he were talking to a person lacking in common sense.

"Some people aren't going to look at it that way," Percy interjected into the father-son conversation. "You helped Helen out by opening the window in her bedroom during a blizzard and uncovering her as she lay in a drunken stupor on her bed. Nature did the rest. In a lot of books, that's second degree murder, gentlemen. The state frowns on people rushing somebody to meet their maker."

"And all this time, Lily thought it was me?" William's voice was filled with wonder.

"This gets better, Bill," said Percy. "Or worse, take your pick. Skip to ten years later and the younger version of Helen, in your father's opinion. A few nights ago Lily and Conrad, her new friend and lover, showed up here."

"He was but one of many, that evil dwarf," Senior Waller interrupted, spitting out the words.

Percy went on as if he hadn't interrupted. "After a few drinks, Lily and Connie talk about having 'relations' in the window of the family jewelry store. Your father overhears them and decides to do something about her behavior. As he had her mother's."

The old man drew back his head, his chin nearly disappearing into his neck. He glanced away and was silent. Hanson looked like he might throw up.

"But Waller's ticker is even in worse shape than ten years ago, so he really needs Hanson's help this time, which he gets in spades. Odds are your father took the gun out of Lily's handbag sometime when they were boozing it up here at the townhouse. He knows she carries, so it couldn't have been too hard to find a moment, right, old man? I'll bet we're going to find your fingerprints all over the inside of her handbag. The cops are checking that now."

She leaned closer to the stiff-backed man, but turned her face, addressing the son.

"When the two lovebirds leave, Frick and Frack here follow them to the jewelry store. They keep an eye on them through the plate glass window. He sees his chance to put the kibosh on the elf when Lily leaves the room to go to the bathroom. Not sure if that was the original plan. Maybe he planned on doing them both in, but this worked just as well. Kill the elf; Lily hangs for the crime. Might be Lily saved her life by going to the john."

Percy stood up straight and looked at William, now pale and shaking. "He returns the revolver to her purse, while Hanson stuffs the body into the display window. It all probably takes less than a minute." Percy wheels around to face the elder man. "How am I doing, old man?" She returns her gaze to William. "After the deed is done, they take off before Lily comes out of the bathroom, leaving her holding the bag; no pun intended. She panics and takes off, which plays perfectly into your father's plan. There was one little problem,

though. Your father and Hanson didn't think anyone else saw them, but they were wrong." She leaned in again, taunting the man.

"Weren't you, old man? A little Christmas angel, on another one of her pilfering missions for a diamond trinket of one sort or another, sees the whole thing, probably crouched down behind one of the counters." Percy straightened up again and turned back to the son.

"Gertie – that's the Christmas angel's name – lets your father know soon afterward what she saw. Like dear old dad, she knows a lethal opportunity when she sees one. She probably demands money or much larger trinkets. And she's not a dummy. She knows she's got a crackerjack blackmail scheme going for herself."

Waller senior shifted uncomfortably in his chair. Hanson, sweat dripping from his brow, turned on him. "I told you we shouldn't hurt her, sir. I told you -"

"Shut up!" Waller didn't look at his servant, as he delivered his edict. "Just shut up."

"Yeah, shut up, Hanson," Percy said, in mock tones. "I'm telling this story and I work solo. Where was I? Oh, yeah. The next night the deadly duo over here agree to meet Gertie at Santa Land round about midnight. Daddy Waller knows all about the tunnels, so they go in the jewelry store and through the tunnels, being real quiet to keep from waking Ernie who's sleeping in the boiler room. They meet Gertie stage left, where Waller delivers a mean blow to the back of her head, probably while the ever-faithful servant here is distracting her. Somewhere in this time frame, he makes a phone call to Rikers Island inciting Danny DeLuca to break out and tail me in the hopes of finding Lily. Hell, you've got a lot of influence. Maybe you bribed a few people to help DeLuca break out. Might be he would do you a favor and follow-up on his promise to kill the girl. I'm sure that was your hope." She

stopped talking and stood in front of the elder man. "I may not have everything in the right order but I think I got it all in, didn't I?"

Mr. Waller rose from his chair in careful, slow movements. Percy stared down at him unflinching. From behind his back he drew out a small derringer and aimed it at the female detective. "Very good. Almost one-hundred percent correct. Not that you'll be able to tell anyone."

"Father! You're admitting to this?" William Waller rose so quickly his chair fell back, landing with a thud on the plush, Persian carpet. Neither his father nor Percy looked in his direction.

"Shut up, William, and let me handle this." Waller Senior continued moving toward Percy.

She backed up, but continued to point the pistol directly at senior Waller. "Don't do anything stupid, old man. I don't have any problem with shooting a mean old bastard like you."

"Nor I you, you fat busybody."

"No," shouted Hanson, from the sidelines. "No sir, no more killing. I'll talk. I swear I will. I'll tell the police what I did, what we did -"

His employer whipped the derringer around and fired once at his servant, the bullet hitting him in the upper chest. Hanson reeled backward from the impact, hit the wall, and slid to the floor. Senior Waller took another aim at the man on the floor.

Before senior Waller could pull the trigger again, Percy fired, the bullet hitting the man's hand. He collapsed into a chair groaning in pain, clutching at his bloody, wounded hand.

A stunned but wordless William walked to his father's side and stood looking down at him. The son reached out a tentative hand then pulled it back, almost as if he'd touched fire. Then he turned to Hanson lying on the floor, taking measured steps to the servant's side.

There was a pounding at the door and the muffled cries of several men.

"What's going on in there? Open up in the name of the law. This is the police."

"They must have heard the shots." Percy pivoted in the direction of the voices. "You'd better get the door, Bill, before they knock it down." There were the sounds of splintering wood, a crash, and then thudding feet coming nearer. "Too late."

Picking up on Percy's calm demeanor, William stooped down and checked Hanson's wound, as three policemen, followed by Hutchers, ran into the room. Percy lowered her gun.

"What the hell?" Hutchers stood in the doorway. He looked from one wounded man to the other.

"She…that woman shot both of us," the old man said. Though his voice cracked, showing his pain, his tone was indignant and accusatory.

"Ooo, what a liar." Percy squashed a hoot of laughter. "True, I shot the old man, Hutchers, but only after he plugged the butler and was about to do it again."

"What she says is true, Detective. My father shot this man." William Waller had more control and authority in his voice than Percy had ever heard. "And he also shot the man my daughter is accused of killing." He could not or would not look at his father.

Hutchers reached for the pistol from Percy's hand. She released her grip on it.

Both she and the detective crossed over to Hanson lying on the floor and bent down. Hutchers examined the wound while Hanson asked in a weak voice, "Am I going to die, sir?"

Hutchers shook his head. "Naw, it went clean through…."

"Yeah, you just might, Hanson," Percy said, making her voice louder than the detective's. "So you might as well make a clean breast of it now. Set the record straight."

"All right." Hanson stuttered. "I will."

"Shut up, Hanson," Waller ordered from his chair at the table.

"Shut up yourself…sir." Hanson's voice was still weak but clear. He looked up at Percy, not seeing one of the officers crossing to Hutchers.

"Ambulance is on its way." The young officer had a decided green tinge to his complexion.

Hutchers glanced up at the rookie policeman standing over him. "I know this is your first crime scene, but take this down, Rogers. It'll be good experience."

"Yes, sir." Rogers withdrew a small notepad from the inside pocket of his uniform with shaky hands. Hutchers turned back to Hanson.

Hutchers nodded and turned back to the man lying on the floor.

"It was just like you said, madam, almost all of it. Mr. Waller shot the funny little man and struck the woman on the head with a brick we found in one of the tunnels. I dragged her body into the little house. She did see Mr. Waller Senior shoot the elf. And I was the one who returned the gun to her handbag before I put it under the body." He turned to Hutchers. "I guess both our fingerprints are in that bag."

Hutchers turned a puzzled face toward Percy, she waggled an eyebrow and then both turned back to the bleeding man on the floor. Hutchers opened his mouth to speak but Percy's voice over road his once more.

"You the one that tried to run me down outside my apartment building in the middle of the night?"

Hanson looked at Percy and nodded. "I was just obeying orders, Miss." He let out a moan and whispered. "But I wasn't trying to hit you, just scare you."

"Tell that to my feet."

"So you're saying the senior Waller over there killed the elf and the Christmas angel, not Lily Waller," interjected Hutchers. "And did so with your help?"

Hanson rolled his eyes and focused on the detective. "Yes, sir, I am. I want to meet my maker with a clear conscience." His head lolled to the side, and he closed his eyes.

"Hey, I thought you said he wasn't going to die." Percy stared at the detective, concern in her voice. Faint sirens sounded. She stood and pivoted in the direction of the wailing.

"The ambulance is almost here." Hutchers put a practiced finger to a pulse point on the man's neck. "He'll be all right. He just passed out. I ain't no doctor, but it looks like the bullet hit some of the muscles in his shoulder and went on through. I don't think it even hit a bone."

"I'm glad to know he'll get the chance to spend the rest of his life in prison. Maybe he can even share a cell with his boss." Percy gestured to Senior Waller.

Hutchers chuckled, stood up, and went over to the old man sitting in the chair. Waller's hand had been wrapped in one of the cloth napkins and his son stood close by, shocked but apparently trying to grapple with what had happened.

"I'm sorry, Bill," Percy said, approaching the jeweler. "It was the only way I could tie this up and get Lily out of jail right away. It was tough on you and I'm sorry." He didn't answer or even look at her. It seemed as if he was frozen in time.

Hutchers glanced down at the old man. "Do you have anything you want to say? Any defense you could possibly offer?"

"Don't be an ass." The man sneered.

"It's Christmas time, you killed an elf and an angel, and I'm the ass?" Hutchers shook his head. "News to me."

"I want to call my lawyer. That woman shot me unprovoked."

"Unprovoked?" His son came to life. William stared at his father, shock turning into disgust. "Father, how many people have you killed? My wife? Lily's boyfriend? Now you shot Hanson and you threatened to shoot Miss Cole? What kind of monster are you?"

"You forgot Gertie," Hutchers offered. "Just to keep the record straight. She was a thief, a blackmailer, and a lousy bookkeeper, but still a human being."

The ever-increasing wail of sirens stopped abruptly. Hutchers beckoned to Officer Rogers, who was never far away. "The ambulance is here, son. Go show them where we are."

Rogers nodded with a half salute and headed for the door. Hutchers walked discretely toward the door, too, but turned back to keep an eye on his shooter. He leaned against the door frame alert, but his eyes half closed, giving William and Percy a modicum of privacy.

William took the moment and gestured for Percy to follow him to the other end of the long table, out of earshot. Once there, he turned to Percy. "How long have you known it was my father?"

"Today for sure."

He dropped into a nearby chair and covered his hands with his face. "I can't believe any of this." Percy was silent, giving the man a chance to talk. "I seem to be surrounded by deceit and lies. My own father. And poor Lily, thinking all these years I killed her mother. And then me, thinking she'd killed that man. You're right. I am a moron. We're a family of morons."

"Look on the bright side. Everybody knows the truth now."

"'*And you will know the truth, and the truth will set you free.*' That's a quote from the Bible."

"I know."

"Long ago, when Lily was a child, I'd take her to Sunday school, and we would read the Bible together. I loved those days."

"Maybe you can get back to them. At least, nobody ever got kicked to the curb for trying."

Chapter Twenty-five

"How are you feeling, Pop? Better I hope." His face no longer appeared fevered but healthier. More energy radiated from him.

"Penicillin is a miracle drug, Persephone. The doctor says the infection is clearing up. It didn't take but overnight for me to start feeling more like my old self again."

"You continue like this, you might make it home for Christmas, Pop. If not, we'll bring it to you. We'll smuggle in Oliver and Fred. You see if we don't."

"Oliver! I miss my grandson every day. You see the pictures that Oliver drew of the new dog for me?" He pointed to a window where several eight by eleven paper-filled drawings were propped up against the glass pane. "The boy's got talent. I was afraid he'd be as bad an artist as your mother, but don't tell her I said that," he added hurriedly.

"Wouldn't dream of it, Pop. I think the only thing Oliver inherited from Mother is his tendency to hum tuneless and annoying little ditties. Better not tell Mother I said *that*."

"Not on your life, Persephone. Let's shake on it." He reached out a hand. They both laughed and shook hands. "Someday I hope we can get rid of all those pictures hanging in the parlor. They give me nightmares. Maybe we can get Oliver to draw something to take their place. There's another thing we probably shouldn't tell your mother."

They were silent for a moment. Pop fiddled with his pillows and Percy sat on the edge of the bed.

"Pop, I want to talk to you," she said, straightening his covers, "Waller didn't cough up the five grand--"

"Well, he didn't have to, Persephone," Pop interrupted. "Not with Lily spending the night in jail like that. All bets were off. I know that upsets your plans, and I'm sorry about that."

"That's all right, Pop." She took a check out of her suit pocket. "He didn't give us the five grand, but he did give us a thousand smackers, as per our agreement that I solve the case." She waved the check in the air. "Look at this. Merry Christmas to the Coles."

Pop took the check from her outstretched hand, a non-committal look crossing his face. "That'll go a long way to you finding a new place for you and Oliver."

"No, Pop, no. It goes into the family coffers. We have running costs. And I think it's time Cole Investigations did a little advertising. Let people know we're around."

"You mean you're not moving out?" His blue eyes got large, happiness dancing inside them.

"Naw, who needs it? I got a good deal going right where I am. Nice people I live with, a little strange, but willing babysitters."

He reached out and stroked her cheek. "You're a good girl, Persephone. A girl can't be as sweet and loving as you and not have someone snatch her up one of these days. You'll find that man and then you and Oliver will have a new home with him. That's the way it should be."

Percy stuck out her hand in a gesture meant to stop the conversation. "Pop, believe it or not, I am content. No more talk about men in or out of my life. My life is good. This is going to be a fine Christmas. I'll take a little of this money and buy Oliver a red Radio Flyer."

"That the wagon he's been wanting?"

"It is, Pop. Between that, the dog, and you getting well, this will be the best Christmas my son's ever had. Actually, all of us." She looked at his face and smiled. "I should go, Pop. You're a little tired."

Pop leaned back and nodded. His turned his head, eyes focusing on a nearby cot, neatly made up with covers and cushions from home.

"Your mother's taken to spending the nights here with me, just like when I first broke my leg. I like that. This place has a nice homey touch, thanks to Mother. She's bringing in some of her ferns from the parlor. She says they have medicinal properties. If nothing else, they'll remind me of home. I'm a lucky man."

"Yeah, you are. We all are, Pop. You rest now."

Her father closed his eyes, and Percy slipped out the door. She took a few steps down the busy hospital corridor and saw Lily sitting on a bench by the elevator, dressed in her dark green coat and hat. She looked calm and serene, not like the first time Percy had seen her wearing the combo.

Lily stood up when Percy approached. The corners of her dark eyes were creased by a broad smile that covered her face. Percy had never seen her smile like that before. She actually looked happy.

"Lily, what a surprise. I'm glad to see you. I know you only got released yesterday but it seems like a long time. How does it feel to be free?"

"It's like being reborn, Percy."

"Well, let's not get carried away."

"No, truly. My life is going to be different from now on. You know, with the baby and all."

They stood smiling at one another for a moment. Percy went on, "I haven't heard from you since I got your note about being released from jail. I wondered what you were up to, but you look like it's okay. Sera packed your things. You can drop by for them any time."

"I'm sorry I didn't come back yesterday, but I've had a lot of things to do."

"Like what?"

Lily didn't answer but took Percy by the arm. "Let's walk a bit."

"Sure."

They began to stroll down the corridor arm in arm like old friends.

"I had a lot of time to think in jail."

"I bet."

"Even one night in jail can change you, Percy."

"Every lifer says that."

"You think about a lot of things. Not just about being free but about money."

"One of my favorite subjects."

Lily stopped walking and turned to face Percy.

"It's not the money you have, but what you do with it."

"That's what they tell me."

Lily laughed. "I was here visiting my doctor, saw your car, and thought I'd wait and see you after you visited your father. Let you know what's going on. But first, how's Pop? I didn't want to barge in and interrupt things."

"Doing good. The penicillin is working and Pop's feeling better. But Pop would love to see you, Lily. Drop by and say hello. He considers you one of the family now."

"Does he? I'm so glad."

"We all do."

"Thank you for saying that."

"It's true or I wouldn't say it. Haven't I always told you like it is?"

"You tell everybody like it is, Percy."

"Yeah, but sometimes I mean it more than other times. I was tough on you in the beginning. For that I apologize."

"Don't. At least you cared enough to be tough. I always knew that."

"Then I guess we've got a warmhearted ending here." She turned and faced the younger woman. "So, Lily, have a great life but don't be a stranger. You're one of those rare commodities, an extended member of the Cole family. We're small but mighty."

"You're not so small, Percy."

Percy stared at her for a split-second. "Holy cripes, did you just make a joke? Don't tell me you have a sense of humor."

"Maybe I've been hanging around you too long."

Both women laughed.

Percy pressed the elevator button, Lily by her side. The detective looked up at the floor indicator, but continued to talk, her voice taking on a more serious tone.

"Pop doesn't know yet you're covering the hospital bills. I didn't tell him, just like you asked in your note. You don't have to do that, you know. But I guess this is one of those 'it's not the money you have, but what you do with it' things."

"You saved my life." Lily's voice choked up and Percy turned to look at her. "If it hadn't been for you, I would be in jail for a crime I didn't commit."

"Sent up the river without a paddle, huh?" Percy said, with a grin. "Somebody else would have rescued you.

"Maybe. No, I don't think so. Nobody else believed I was innocent, not even my father. Nobody knew me, inside. Just you and your family. That's all I had. Not that I blame Dad or anybody else, considering how I've behaved in the past."

She looked down at her hands. Aside from a dark green leather clutch bag, she carried a small package and played nervously with the cord wrapped around the brown paper.

"As Oliver says, Lily, we all make mistakes. It's too bad about your grandfather, but the man is no better than a Nazi Storm Trouper. From what I can tell, he's had this sort of mentality all his life. Remember that. It'll help you get through. Also remember you're better off without him."

Lily didn't reply for a moment then nodded her head slowly. "I know. It's tougher on Dad, but he say this explains a lot about the past."

"Bill turned out to be all right. And he found his backbone, too. Your father never once flinched at spilling everything to the cops when the time came. I hope you give him a chance to make this up to you. He does love you, you know."

"I will." She gave a faint smile and took a deep breath. "Remember that day in the kitchen? When I told you I hated my life? You told me to change it. So I am. Besides the baby, I've decided to open a cooking school. Dad says he wants to be a part of it."

"A cooking school? But you already know how to cook. I'm carrying around an extra five pounds of fat to prove it."

"This is much bigger. There's a new building at Columbus Circle. I bought it. I'm hiring famous French chefs, all refuges, and bringing them over to America to give people classes in gourmet cooking. It's a fairly new concept, called haute cuisine. Not what I do, which is plain, old American cooking."

"But delicious," Percy put in.

"Thank, you." Lily chuckled. "I think you've been my best customer. After the school opens, I hope to take a few of these classes myself. You wouldn't believe what's coming out of France now, even with the war on, and so many talented chefs have been displaced."

"And you're going to place them. Clever girl."

The elevator arrived and the doors opened with a dinging sound. The two women stepped forward into the empty car and the doors closed.

"Another elevator without an operator." Percy stood with her hands on her hips. "I can't get used to these things. I hope we get to where we want to go." Percy pressed the main floor button.

"This is for you, Percy." Lily thrust the package in her hand once the car started moving. "Merry Christmas."

"You didn't have to do this," Percy protested, unwrapping the brown paper. The glittering chainmail of the small evening bag felt soft and smooth in her hands, not at all like she expected metal to feel. She stared at the intricately carved green dragon, with the sparkling ruby eyes. "Holy Toledo! It's gorgeous! I didn't realize Evidence released it."

"They gave it back to me this morning. I had it cleaned before I wrapped it."

"This is for me? You can't give me this."

"Yes, I can; we're extended family. Besides, the bag seems more you than me. I've seen you in that Japanese bathrobe your mother made. And don't you wear a lot of green?"

"I have my Sunday Go To Meeting green suit. I wear that about twice a year. Except for that robe, I don't wear colors as a rule, just black and white."

"You should. Try wearing green, pink or bright blue instead; something colorful. Nearly everything would look grand with your hair. You'd sizzle, as a cook might say."

The elevator car landed on the ground floor with a slight thud and the doors opened. The women emerged, moving quickly aside to let six new elevator riders in.

"I've got to go," Lily said, putting her hand lightly on Percy's. "A meeting with Immigration on bringing some of the chefs here. The ones that are Jewish and Polish are taking precedence, but they all need my help. Thank you again for helping *me*. I'll come by and visit Pop tomorrow morning. Promise." She turned hurriedly to leave, glancing at her wrist watch, before she took long, purposeful strides to the exit doors.

"You're so grown up," Percy marveled, calling after her. "When did that happen?"

Lily's hand flew to her abdomen, as she wheeled around, pausing for a moment. "Someone has to be the grownup and I'm the one having the baby."

She spun around again, coat fluttering in a full circle, and ran out the door.

Percy stood for a moment, staring after the girl's departing figure. Then she looked down at the bag in her hand, far more elegant and luxurious than anything she'd ever owned.

"Where'd you get that purse, Perce?"

Even if she hadn't recognized the voice, the 'double purse' remark would have told her. She turned in the direction of his voice and smiled. He was wearing the same beat up hat, but a new trench coat over a dark blue suit.

"Hey, Hutchers. Lily gave it to me for Christmas. What are you doing here?"

"I called your apartment. Sera told me you were here." He removed his hat and rolled it back and forth in his hands. "Wanted to talk to you in person." He paused.

"So talk."

"You're one smart cookie, Perce." Hutchers stared at her with open admiration. "How'd you figure it out? Just like you said, the prints inside the purse were the old man's and Hanson's. Proof positive. That's why we released the bag. We didn't know whose they were until this morning, but sure enough, old man Waller and his accomplice. You nailed it."

"You saying thank you?" She took a step back and stared at the man, a broad grin covering her face.

"I suppose I am."

"Just doing my job." She moved toward the door, still smiling. "You release Harry's son yet?"

"Yeah, although, he's got to have a couple of tests to make sure he's not too mental to be out there. You know, public welfare."

"From what Harry tells me, he and his wife are going to put Ernie in some place called Cypress Haven down in Florida. That might solve the problem."

"Thanks. I'll let the state psychiatrist know."

"Two thank yous in one meeting. This must be a record. Well, I got to fly, Hutchers. Get back to the office, do some shopping, deposit a check at the bank, stuff like that. See you around." She pushed open the exit door but was stopped by his voice.

"Perce, wait up."

She continued passing through the double doors, pausing on the other side. He followed. Percy waited near a signpost right outside Emergency reading, 'No stopping, No kidding'.

"Okay, what's on your mind?"

"You own a dress?"

"What do you mean, do I 'own a dress'?" She didn't bother to conceal the huffiness in her voice. "Sure, I got a dress. What do you take me for, a hillbilly? What's the matter with you?"

She stared at him as her mind flitted back to the formal senior prom dress at the back of the closet, the one she tried on from time to time, covered with a white sheet to keep it from getting dusty.

Come to think of it, it's green. Emerald green, they call it. Jeesh, that thing cost a fortune, over ten bucks, and I only wore it once. I bet if I take all the bows off, I could wear it again.

"No, I don't mean a regular dress," he said, interrupting her thoughts. "I mean a fancy dress. You know long, something for a fancy evening."

"What are you talking about? What do I need a long dress for?"

Hutchers crumpled his hat between his massive hands. "I was wondering if you…you see, there's this thing…"

"Thing?"

"A dance. There's the New Year's Eve Ball. It's a policeman's benefit for widows and orphans kind of thing."

"A widows and orphans kind of thing."

"Naw, you don't want to go," he muttered, turning away.

"Who says I don't want to go?" Percy put a hand on her hip, a belligerence coming into her voice. "If you're going to ask me to go, ask me to go, for crying out loud."

"Okay, I'm asking," he said facing her again and matching her belligerent tone.

"Okay, I'm going," she retorted.

Hutchers mouth dropped open. "You are?"

"Well, do you want me to go or not?"

"Sure I do."

"Okay."

"Okay."

He slapped the crumpled hat on his head repeating the word, but in a gentler tone. "Okay. I'll pick you up New Year's Eve, seven-thirty sharp. And wear high heels. I like my women tall." He gave her a wide grin, added a wink, and turned away, striding into the parking lot.

She watched him depart for a moment then cupped her hands to her mouth and yelled, "You could work on your courting skills."

He laughed, twisted his body around, and walked backward, while shouting, "And you know what you could work on?" He paused for a moment. "Not one damned thing. I like you just the way you are!"

He pivoted back and crossed the parking lot to his car. Percy, mouth opened, gaped after him until his car pulled out and disappeared. Then Persephone Cole began to giggle, something she hadn't done since high school.

Well, Merry Christmas to me. Maybe I'm not such a fat old broad, after all. And if I am, I still got it.

~

Read on for a taste of
Book Three of the
Persephone Cole Vintage Mysteries

The Chocolate Kiss-Off

Chapter One

Dear Diary,

July 15th, 1941. I will always remember this date. This is the day I found out her name, who she is. When I come face to face with her, will she know who I am? Will she be sorry? I will make sure of it, if it takes years.

Chapter Two

"Persela! Persela!"

The banging on the front door merged with the crying of a familiar voice. The sound shot through the thin walls of the apartment like a police siren blaring across forty-second street.

Though it was four forty-five a.m. on a Friday morning, Persephone "Percy" Cole sat bolt up-right, wide awake, and mind alert. She threw back the covers, leapt out of bed, snatched her robe from the end post, and raced out of the room. No time for slippers or pushing long, flaming-red hair out of her face.

The bedroom was the largest of the four in the railroad apartment, but no one else in the family wanted it. Day or night you could hear every noise in the hallway. But Percy Cole, one of Manhattan's first female detectives, liked being the first to know what was what. It suited her.

Reaching the front door within seconds, she grabbed the knob, just as the thumping and calling increased in volume. Without hesitation, Percy flung the door open wide. The only person in the world that called her Persela was Mrs. Goldberg.

The long-time family friend and neighbor froze at the door's opening, a fisted hand drawn back midair. More than a foot shorter than Percy, the older woman threw back her head and looked up, open-mouthed. Words formed on the woman's lips but no sound came forth.

Fear or something closer to horror tracked itself across her face, and came to a stop in pale blue eyes. Percy's own green ones became sharp and searching.

"You'd better get in here, Mrs. Goldberg, and tell me what's wrong."

The five-foot eleven-inch woman stepped aside to allow the rotund one entrance to the apartment. But instead of moving, Mrs. Goldberg picked up the two bottom corners of the long, bibbed apron she was wearing and chucked them over her head.

Bursting into tears, she stood weaving in the doorway. Percy reached down and wrapped a strong arm around the hooded woman, guiding her into the most cluttered room of the lower east side apartment, the parlor-slash-office.

Fast movements returned the detective to the front door, where she gave a quick glance in both directions to see if any neighbors came out into the hall, curious about the commotion. Satisfied the answer was 'no', Percy shut the door. Another glance down the hallway of the apartment showed the doors to her son, sister, and parents' bedrooms all remained closed.

Good. I don't know what the hell's going on, but I don't want to be interrupted yet.

Mrs. Goldberg was where she'd been left, sniffling in the center of the parlor. With gentle fingers, Percy lifted the apron from the top of the weeping woman's head, causing tufts of salt and pepper hair to stick out every which way in the process. She studied the round face, red from crying.

"Sit down, Mrs. Goldberg. You don't look so good."

"How can I look good? My boy's in jail."

Shock colored Percy's voice. "Who's in jail? Howie?"

"How many boys do I have?" Mrs. Goldberg's exasperation overrode her fear.

"What happened?"

"He's been arrested!"

"Howie? Our Howard Goldberg? There's got to be some mistake."

Percy stifled the urge to laugh when she saw the older woman's distressed expression. She waited for Mrs. Goldberg to say more. But instead, the woman let out a wail. It ended in a screech similar to a beginner's violin being played by one of the neighborhood kids.

Percy hurried to close the parlor door, hoping the rest of the family would remain sleeping, although things were getting dicier by the minute. She turned back to the wobbly woman.

"You need to sit, Mrs. Goldberg, before you fall down."

When she got no response, Percy took the woman by the elbow and led her to the faded brocade sofa dominating the section of the room nearest the door. She repeated the command in a tone usually saved for the family dog.

"Sit." Percy gave a gentle push.

Still sobbing, Mrs. Goldberg fell on the sofa, let out a hiccup, and wiped her nose on the edge of the apron. Percy eased into the matching overstuffed chair, and leaned forward.

"You look like you could use something to calm your nerves. Mother's sherry? Sweet but soothing." She gestured to a half-filled bottle of sherry perched on the radio console at the end of the sofa. "Or Pop's whiskey? Strong but numbing." She studied her friend and neighbor.

"Whiskey it is."

Percy patted the other woman's hand in an encouraging manner, stood, and disappeared behind a gold and cobalt blue screen covered with strutting, iridescent peacocks. As far as Percy was concerned, the screen was an unwelcomed legacy from a deceased great-aunt, but her mother loved it. As it served to separate the Cole Brothers Detective Agency from the family parlor, Percy chose to ignore the tasteless addition to an already crowded room.

Mrs. Goldberg let out another sob before the words tumbled out. "He called me from the police station. My Howie! Arrested for murder! *Oy vey iz mir!*"

"Murder? In that case, I could use something, myself. You take a couple of deep breaths while I'm pouring," Percy said from behind the screen. The sounds of a drawer opening, a top being unscrewed from a bottle, and a quick pour into two glasses could be heard. "Start at the beginning."

"What beginning?" Mrs. Goldberg's voice trembled on the other side of the barrier. "Who knows the beginning? He calls and tells me he found a dead woman in the chocolate this morning when he gets to work and when he tells the police, they arrest him, my Howie, for murder."

She was silent. Even her breathing seemed to stop.

Percy returned from behind the screen carrying two full shot glasses. She shoved one in Mrs. Goldberg's hand, who sat in a daze.

"Go on, drink that," Percy said, swallowing about half of the amber liquid in her own glass in one gulp. "Good stuff," she muttered in appreciation.

She sat down again opposite Mrs. Goldberg, who took a tentative sip of the alcohol and coughed. But the woman's color returned and Percy was satisfied. She leaned in again.

"Okay, so Howie found a dead woman?"

Mrs. Goldberg nodded vehemently. "Yes. Persela, he says the police, they think he killed this woman he found in the chocolate. But you know my Howie; he wouldn't hurt a fly, such a gentle boy, such a good boy, always remembering my birthday and so kind to animals. All the ones he would bring home to doctor and take care of, years and years of them. You remember those pigeons, flying all over the apartment. Such messy birds, pigeons. I was covered in pigeon droppings for weeks."

"At the chocolate factory, right?"

"The pigeons?"

"The body."

"Yes, yes. *Oy,* those pigeons. Remember?"

"Forget the pigeons."

Mrs. Goldberg wiped her eyes and went on, not hearing Percy's comment.

"But could you tell that boy anything? No. Three baby birds he carried with him wherever he went for nearly a month. He nursed them back to health no matter what anybody said," Mrs. Goldberg added, with a touch of pride.

The memory of Howie as a nine-year old boy flashed through Percy's mind. Howard Goldberg - Howie to his friends and family -- was a true *mensch*, Yiddish for an all-around good guy. He was not only a dear friend, but also godfather to her son. As far as Percy was concerned Captain America had nothing on him.

"When did Howie call you from the police station? What time?"

"Who could know the time? I was making the *Challah* for the store, like I do every day, that's all I know. He said he didn't want me to hear it on the radio. Who plays the radio? All I hear about is that Hitler and Benny Goodman. Then he said I was the only call he could make, so to be sure to run up and get you."

"That would be Howie who called you."

"Who else? Hitler?"

"Just clarifying, Mrs. Goldberg." Percy took the nearly full shot glass from Mrs. Goldberg's hand and placed it on the side table, while the woman continued talking.

"And what does that mean; I'm the 'only call'? Are they charging money to make these phone calls? I told him to always carry a dollar on him, always, but does he listen? No, I'm just his mother. You never know when you're going to need money for an emergency, like now." She started to sob again, and picked up the corners of her soggy apron, dabbing at her eyes.

Percy's mind raced, paying little attention to Mrs. Goldberg's chidings of her son's disregard for a mother's golden words.

"Did he say which station he was at?"

Mrs. Goldberg didn't answer, but shook her head. She became distracted and over-wrought again, her face taking on a pleading look. Her hands clasped together in a prayer-like manner.

"Persela, help my boy. You're a detective with a badge --"

"A license," Percy murmured, deep in thought.

"A license, a badge, who cares, and so what?" Anger and indignation flared up in Mrs. Goldberg, replacing the fear. "You know he didn't do this. Him! As if he would put somebody in his vat of chocolate like a bon-bon. Not my Howie. It takes him hours and hours to make his chocolate. He's so proud of it. Why just the other day --"

"Forget the chocolate."

"Forget the chocolate, forget the pigeons. Such fuss."

"Right now we need to find him. If we're not careful, he could get lost within the system for days. You're sure he didn't say where he was?"

Percy stood and looked down at her neighbor. The woman stared back, unblinking.

"He lives and works in Brooklyn." Percy answered herself. "Let's see." Percy scrunched her forehead in thought. "He's probably being held at the closest precinct to the factory. That would be the Ninetieth. Did he mention Williamsburg? The Ninetieth?"

"I don't know. Maybe." Mrs. Goldberg looked startled. "The Ninetieth? There are ninety police stations in Brooklyn? It's just a little burg. What kind of dangerous place is that, there should be so many police stations?"

"Forget the police stations."

"*Oy*, so much to forget, who can remember?"

"I'll start with the Ninetieth," Percy said more to herself than Mrs. Goldberg. "With any luck, he's there. Then I'll phone Jude." Percy noticed the terrified look returning to the other woman's face. "Don't worry. It'll be all right. We'll get him out of this."

It was a large promise, but even without any facts, Percy knew one thing. While anyone is capable of murder given the right circumstances, the Howard Goldberg she knew would never kill someone and put them in a vat of chocolate. To him chocolate was sacrosanct. Percy looked down at Howie's mother.

"You okay? You want to lie down for a moment?"

Mrs. Goldberg shook her head, caught up in her thoughts. Percy studied her with sympathy.

That's how I'd be if my son got arrested for murder.

"Here's an idea." Percy leaned down and stroked the woman lightly on the shoulder to get her attention. "Why don't you go to the kitchen and rustle us up some coffee? I'll make a few calls to see what's going on. You know where everything is, right?"

Mrs. Goldberg rallied, stood, and smoothed out her apron. "Better than your mother, Persela. How she can find anything the way she keeps that kitchen of hers, I'll never know, but I'm not one to complain."

"You? Never."

"Of course, this room has so much gold paint it's enough to wake the de..." Mrs. Goldberg broke off speaking as suddenly as she'd started. "What am I doing, talking about paint when my son..." She brought one hand to her face, pressing fingers against quivering lips.

"Easy, Mrs. Goldberg."

Percy put a sturdy arm around the short woman's shoulders again. Mrs. Goldberg leaned into her, looking small, fragile and old. Percy hated seeing her like that.

"We'll find out what's what and take care of it. You go make that coffee. Mr. Goldberg still out of town?"

"My Seymour comes back from sitting Shiva tomorrow. Seven whole days he's been in the Bronx. How will I tell him?" Mrs. Goldberg's entire body began to tremble. "First, my Seymour's brother dead from cancer and now this! Our Howie!" She shook her head sadly, moving with heavy steps toward the door. "I'll go make with the coffee."

Percy watched her go out the door then turned. She headed again to the corner of the room where the Cole Brothers Investigations office resided. Behind the screen, two small dark oak desks sat, one belonging to her, the other to her father.

Sitting down, she opened her desk drawer, pulled out the phone book, looked up the Brooklyn police station in question, and dialed the number. Even though it was barely five o'clock in the morning, the phone answered on the first ring.

"Ninetieth Precinct. Officer O'Hara speaking."

Percy heard a world of attitude in those few brief words. Officer O'Hara sounded young, yet already jaded. The low-income residential and factory district had high crime and little love for coppers. It turned even rookies into worn-out cynics fast.

"Good morning." Percy tried to make her voice sound business-like but polite. "I'm looking for a Howard Goldberg and wondered if he was brought there this morning? Maybe an hour or two ago."

"Who wants to know? This his wife?"

If I say I'm a private detective, there's going to be twenty minutes of crapola and then he'll only hang up on me.

"Yeah, I'm his wife. Is he there? He called his mother but didn't call me, the louse."

"A real mama's boy, huh? Yeah, we got him."

"What's the charge?"

"We're holding him for questioning on suspicion of murder."

"On what grounds?"

"On the grounds of the victim got found in a big bowl of his chocolate with a rope around her neck pulled tighter than my mother's girdle. You'd better get a lawyer, lady. It don't look so good for him."

"If he's around, I'd like to talk to him."

"Naw. He's in his cell by now. It being Friday, he won't be arraigned until Monday morning. He'll be spending the weekend in the slammer. Don't worry, we'll treat him right, honey." Officer O'Hara left off with a laugh indicating just the opposite.

"Thanks." She hung up then muttered, "And don't call me honey."

Percy reached into the top drawer and snatched a stick of Doublemint gum from a pack. Opening it up, she folded the gum into a wad and shoved it in her mouth, chewing absentmindedly.

It was an old trick her father showed her years ago to keep Mother from knowing he 'tipped the bottle' from time to time. Mother tipping the sherry bottle never seemed to count.

She dialed her brother, Jude, and looked around at the cramped quarters as the phone rang. Two file cabinets, worn but cared-for, were crammed against the wall into a space too small for the amount of business they were currently doing. She let out a sigh.

Percy grew up with the room functioning as the office for the detective agency started by her father and uncle. Uncle Gil's sudden death and Pop's recent broken leg had taken their toll on business. Cole Brothers Investigations – once thriving – had receded more and more into a corner of the parlor.

When Percy got her investigator's license six-months earlier, she assumed the lost partnership position. Despite many people's initial scorn of a female detective, the business was resurrecting itself.

Pop was gone on a big case in New Jersey, and she was juggling two other cases, one arriving only the day before. Percy wasn't sure how she'd fit Mrs. Goldberg in, but she'd do more than that; it would take precedence over the other jobs she had going.

Shame to toss them aside, though. Good money. And they're both mostly legwork. Time to spread out and make some changes.

Her brother, Jude, finally answered on the eighth ring. He didn't sound as wide awake as Officer O'Hara, but he didn't sound as jaded, either.

Books by Heather Haven

The Alvarez Family Murder Mysteries
Murder is a Family Business, Book 1
A Wedding to Die For, Book 2
Death Runs in the Family, Book 3
DEAD...If Only, Book 4
The CEO Came DOA, Book 5
The Culinary Art of Murder, Book 6

The Lee Alvarez Mystery Novelettes
Honeymoons Can Be Murder, Book 1
Marriage Can Be Murder, Book 2 (October 2017)

The Persephone Cole Vintage Mysteries
The Dagger Before Me, Book 1
Iced Diamonds, Book 2
The Chocolate Kiss-Off, Book 3

Noir Mystery Stand Alone
Death of a Clown

Collection of Short Stories
Corliss and Other Award-Winning Stories

Multi-Author Boxed Sets
Sleuthing Women: 10 First-in-Series Mysteries
Sleuthing Women II: 10 Mystery Novellas

About Heather Haven

After studying drama at the University of Miami in Miami, Florida, Heather went to Manhattan to pursue a career. There she wrote short stories, novels, comedy acts, television treatments, ad copy, commercials, and two one-act plays, produced at several places, such as Playwrights Horizon. Once she even ghostwrote a book on how to run an employment agency. She was unemployed at the time.

One of her first paying jobs was writing a love story for a book published by Bantam called *Moments of Love*. She had a deadline of one week but promptly came down with the flu. Heather wrote "The Sands of Time" with a raging temperature, and delivered some pretty hot stuff because of it. Her stint at New York City's No Soap Radio - where she wrote comedic ad copy – help develop her long-time love affair with comedy.

She has won five awards so far for the humorous Alvarez Family Murder Mysteries. The Persephone Cole Vintage Mysteries and *Corliss and Other Award Winning Stories* have garnered several, as well.

However, her proudest achievement is winning the Independent Publisher Book Awards (IPPY) 2014 Silver Medal for her stand-alone noir mystery, **Death of a Clown**. As the real-life daughter of Ringling Brothers and Barnum and Bailey circus folk, she was inspired by stories told throughout her childhood by her mother, a trapeze artist and performer. The book cover even has a picture of her mother sitting atop an elephant from that time. Her father trained the elephants. Heather brings the daily existence of the Big Top to life during World War II, embellished by her own murderous imagination.

Connect with Heather at the following sites:

Website: **www:heatherhavenstories.com**
Heather's Blog:
 http://heatherhavenstories.com/blog/
https://www.facebook.com/HeatherHavenStories
https://www.twitter.com/Twitter@HeatherHaven

Sign up for Heather's newsletter at:
http://heatherhavenstories.com/subscribe-via-email/

Email: **heather@heatherhavenstories.com**.

She'd love to hear from you. Thanks so much!

The Wives of Bath Press

The Wife of Bath was a woman of a certain age, with opinions, who's on a journey. Heather Haven and Baird Nuckolls are modern day Wives of Bath.

www.thewivesofbath.com

www.ingramcontent.com/pod-product-compliance
Lightning Source LLC
Chambersburg PA
CBHW071527110726
47908CB00003B/965